MALIBU SERIES
BOOK THREE

IT
STARTED
IN
VENICE

J. J. Sorel

Copyright © April 2021 J. J. Sorel

ALL RIGHTS RESERVED

No part of this book may be reproduced or transmitted in any form, including electronic or mechanical, without written permission from the publisher, except in the case of brief quotations embodied in reviews or articles. This is a work of fiction. Names, characters, businesses, events and incidents are pure product of the author's imagination. Any resemblance to actual persons, living or dead, or an actual event is purely coincidental and does not assume any responsibility for author or third-party websites or content therein.

Cover MOI

Line Edit/proof Wolfsparrow Publishing

"The very essence of romance is uncertainty." **Oscar Wilde**

1

HARRIET

"How could you get married without me there on the wings: crying, cheering, getting drunk, and embarrassing you?" I asked with my hands on my hips.

Hanging her clothes in a walk-in wardrobe as large as my bedroom, Miranda giggled. "It came as a total surprise for me, too."

"But what about a reception? The white dress? Me as your maid of honor, behaving badly and flirting with the best man? The male strip-show for our bachelorette's night? You've really let us down, Sis. And Mom's going crazy."

"Yeah, I know." She sighed.

Miranda had only just returned from Las Vegas and broke the jaw-dropping news that she'd swapped the surname Flowers for Peace.

At first, I'd joked that Flowers and Peace combined sounded very hippie should she decide to hyphenate her surname. But then it hit me: my sister had married filthy rich Lachlan Peace.

My ordinary suburban sister would now call Malibu her home and rub shoulders with the well-heeled, botoxed wealthy.

"We're going to Mom and Dad's for dinner tonight. I'm sure they'll be fine," she said, forcing a smile.

"Mom sounded pretty pissed off on the phone. She wanted to meet Lachlan first and give you her approval," I said, chuckling at how ridiculously old-fashioned that was.

"Isn't it the father who's meant to approve?" she asked.

"Mom wears the pants in the family, so it's kind of the same." I imagined my mother asking all kinds of ridiculous questions like 'what type of books does he read?'

Dazzled by the red velvet dress hanging on Miranda's arm, I said, "That's gorgeous. I'd love to borrow it sometime."

"I was married in it. I'll have to show you the photos. It really was quite strange, if not memorable." She shook her head with a smile that seemed permanent. "We are planning on having a proper wedding, though."

"Oh, great. You mean in a church, followed by a big boozy reception?"

She laughed. "I haven't given it much thought." Rosy-cheeked and eyes beaming, Miranda was no longer that geeky younger sister but a woman of the world.

I glanced down at my watch. "I better get back to the boy. Now that we're neighbors, I can pop in. And maybe stay occasionally?"

Miranda nodded. "I can't see why not. It's such a huge house. I keep getting lost."

I picked up a teddy and raised an eyebrow. "Sexy."

She removed it from my hand and blushed. "Lachlan's got a thing for lacy lingerie."

"Show me a hot-blooded male who hasn't," I said, thinking of Orlando and his juvenile obsession with asking me what color panties I wore.

"Where's Lachlan?"

"At the beach. He's addicted to surfing."

"I went for a swim yesterday," I said. "I'm starting to get healthy. I'll need to cut the cigarettes, though. But it's not easy around Orlando. He likes to smoke."

"But you're his nurse," Miranda said with a note of disapproval. "Is he taking hard drugs, too?"

I smiled at her worried frown. "No. Just a little weed and beer. His parents don't know. We only have the odd one. At night. In the garden."

Miranda stopped what she was doing and looked at me. "How is it going there with him, really?"

I shrugged. "He's up and down." I chuckled. "Not in that way." I tilted my head down to my groin. "He's extremely moody."

"I got your meaning first time, Harry. Not everything has a sexual connotation."

"It has with Orlando. He's pretty frisky."

"You're not leading him on, I hope? You're not wearing that tight little nurse's outfit you recently spoke of."

I grinned at that suggestion. The thought of wearing something skimpy around him raised my temperature.

"No way. I have to behave professionally." I smirked. "He'd love it, though."

"I bet he would." She opened a drawer and filled it with underwear. "I really like the hot pink and purple streaks in your hair. You're not cutting it?"

"I'm growing it out." I hid the fact that Orlando liked long hair. Miranda needn't know of my Orlando obsession, despite me convincing myself that it was just a crush.

"It's his birthday next week. They're arranging a big party."

"That sounds like fun," she said.

The lush garden caught my eye, and I sauntered over to the balcony for a better view of the sprawling, well-manicured grounds. I thought of our earlier visits when Ava chased butterflies and picked flowers.

As I braced the marble balustrade, salty air grazed my face. I couldn't quite fathom that this massive estate was now Miranda's home. Our mom would approve. She'd always aspired to hobnob it with the rich, on the proviso they were cultivated and well-educated.

"I have to pick up Ava later today," I said, stepping back inside.

"Mom's dying to homeschool her," Miranda said.

"That's not going to happen. She loves going to school. She's such a social girl. Which is healthy, don't you think?"

"Sure do. She's a friendly little girl."

"Do you think Ava can stay here? Since it's the weekend."

Miranda nodded. "I can't see why not. They have dance classes in the morning. And Manuel always loves her being around. They can practice."

I smiled, thinking of my little angel. "They're so talented, aren't they? She's going to be a star. I just know it."

"Mom's hating it, of course. She wants Ava to take up science or something sensible," Miranda said, unzipping her skirt.

"My god, you've lost weight."

"I have a little." She smiled.

"All that exercise in bed, ah?" I grinned.

"Uh-huh."

"I need to work out what to do." I sighed. "It's become a seven-day-a-week job. Clarissa even suggested I move in."

Miranda's eyes widened. "Really? In the cottage with Orlando?"

I laughed. "You make it seem as though I'm a lamb moving into a lion's den."

"Almost." She removed her shoes.

"There's a cottage next to Orlando's."

"It sounds like a good arrangement to me." Miranda held a pair of bikinis.

"Are you going to the beach?" I asked.

"I thought I'd go down for a dip." She wiped her brow. "It's so warm."

"Woo-hoo. Aren't we living the high life?" I chuckled. "Anyway, I thought about it, and I'm moving in. We'll be neighbors."

"Does the family know about Ava?"

"They're totally cool about her moving in. They're so generous." I sighed.

"Then what's the issue?" she asked. "Ava would love it. And she can come here as often as she likes."

"I'd have to change schools. And I'm not sure how long we'll be staying."

"Then arrange for her to go to Manuel's school," she said.

"Mm... maybe. But it may only be a few months. Won't that be disruptive?"

"I need to go to the Artefactory every day, which means I can take Ava to school. And on those days when I can't, I'm sure you could arrange something," Miranda said, changing into her bikini. "We can take it in turns."

"That would work for sure. And this will be such an amazing experience for Ava." I stared down at my hands. "I just hope I'm up to it."

Orlando's temperamental moods had me on the hop. I couldn't blame him for acting like a spoiled brat. If I was paralyzed, I would have thrown tantrums. Just like he did over silly things, like running out of beer or his favorite chips. The type of pathetic behavior that normally I'd roll my eyes at. But I no longer recognized myself as I tiptoed around him.

Miranda put her arm around me. "What's wrong?"

"All this change, I suppose." I shrugged. "Ava will love it here, to be sure. But what happens when we revert to our ordinary life in that tiny apartment?"

"Ava can always come here on weekends. This is my home. You're family. And I love Ava."

I hugged her and instantly all my nagging issues were replaced by a head rush as I pictured myself in Miranda's large swimming pool, adrift on an inflatable chair, sipping a cocktail.

"I better get back. I'll speak to Clarissa about us moving in. Even if it's only a brief stay. It's still exciting."

"And what about the condo, will you let it go?" Miranda said.

I shrugged. "I might as well. I'll be here for a few months. At the most."

"At the most?" Her eyebrows knitted. "So, you really think Orlando might walk again?"

"I'm not sure, but the doctors seem hopeful." I touched her hand. "Hey, thanks for offering to help with Ava. Should I wait until you've spoken to Lachlan before bringing her here after school?"

"No need."

She walked me to the door.

"See you later, then," I said, kissing her on the cheek.

She waved, and I headed back to Orlando Thornhill's sprawling estate.

2

ORLANDO

Flexing my foot while gritting my teeth, I tried to lengthen my leg. I had to pinch my lips to stifle a groan. My disconnected brain had beaten me again, and I slumped in my chair to catch my breath. Exercise used to bore me. Now, it frustrated the crap out of me. I had sure as hell taken my body for granted.

Thanks to Harriet's unwavering attention, which I likened to that of a bossy boot camp instructor, I'd developed some movement in my legs. Considering how lifeless they'd been for the past few months, the fact that I could move them at all was a fucking miracle.

"Darling, you're doing so well." My mother's lips trembled. Something she did when about to cry.

My dad squeezed my shoulder. "We're really proud of you."

For the first time in months, I cracked a smile. My legs weren't the only dormant part of my anatomy. My face ached from having remained deadpan for months.

"Harry's helped. She pushes me to do my exercises." I puffed a breath. "I haven't exactly been a bundle of laughs."

My mother smiled sadly. "We'd love to host a party for you. But only if you feel like it."

"Why not? Should be fun," I lied.

Despite the skin-crawling dread at seeing pity in people's eyes, I had to man up and ditch the shitty mood. I had to be that anything-goes dude again, despite the former shallow version, which now stalked my nightmares, a stranger to me.

Harriet understood. I could let it all hang out around her. That's why I needed her here. Pretending was as torturous as stretching my legs.

While my mom fussed about, my father picked up my guitar and played soothing cords. Like a bird singing in the dark, my dad's gentle strums comforted me. I'd grown up with him strumming in the garden, around the pool, and everywhere.

I first learned to play music while on his lap.

"Are you practicing?" he asked.

I nodded. "Harry makes me pick it up."

He frowned. "You need someone to push you?"

How could I tell him that some days I felt like shit and just wanted to crawl under a rock?

My mom bent down and cuddled me. "You're doing so well with your exercises. There's such a vast improvement. You can actually move your legs. That's extraordinary progress."

A knock came at the door. I felt a spark and my mood lifted as Harriett entered. I glanced at my mother and wondered if she'd noticed. She didn't normally miss a thing.

From the moment I lost the use of my legs, my parents hovered around more than usual. I understood why. They loved me. And

I loved them just as much. I just craved space, so I could perv on Harriet, flirt, and be dirty.

That's why I'd asked them to employ her. I needed a pretty face and a hot body to lift my spirits. And she did that all right with her tight tank tops and jeans that hugged her perfect ass.

She thought I'd forgotten. I hadn't.

It started in Venice. This obsession with my nurse. Fucking in a rundown apartment with Harriet had been hotter than waking to a million-dollar view with a girl rummaging through a Louis Vuitton bag.

One of the many advantages of being a musician and born into money were the endless girls.

My dick still functioned. But who would want me now?

I should have told Harriet I'd remembered hooking up. She wasn't the kind of woman one easily forgot. A part of me felt bad for not contacting her after that one night together. I wanted to. But then life swept me away.

"Hey, everyone," Harriet sang, setting her bag down.

My mother said, "Orlando's improved so much."

Harriet nodded. "He's making fine progress. The doctors are pleased."

"That's wonderful," my mom replied with a bright smile directed at me.

My dad turned to Harriet. "You're a great help and support."

"I'm glad to be of service. And it's such a beautiful place here." Harriet tapped her belly. "And the food's really nice. I'm stacking on the weight."

In all the right places.

"I'm glad you've decided to move into the cottage."

Harriet cast me a side-glance before returning to my mother. "Are you sure you don't mind my five-year-old daughter being here, too?"

"We'd love to see a little one running around," my father said.

"I'll send Mary to make sure it's comfortable for you," my mom added.

"It's really fine as it is. Don't go to any trouble."

After my parents left, I said, "Since you're moving in, I can wheel over and annoy you."

"You'd never annoy me, Orlando." She tilted her head and then turned to the window. "Is the ramp built yet? I thought we could go down to the beach later."

"Only if you promise to wear your skimpiest bikini," I said.

Harriet rolled her eyes. Always the professional, I didn't recognize that wild girl I'd met at the Red House. I missed her. But I understood she had a job to do.

"The ramp's ready. We'll go later, if you like," I said, watching her flick open her pad. "Is that your list of sadistic activities?"

Harriet cocked her head. "You wish."

I laughed. She brightened my day. "Hey, how about we get together tonight to celebrate?"

"What are we celebrating?"

"You becoming my neighbor."

She shrugged. "Sure. Why not? Ava's staying at Miranda's over the weekend while I get set up."

"Cool. We can hang out. And you won't even have to play nursie. Although, I don't mind you playing her. I'm just hanging out for the uniform." I grinned.

Harriet placed her hands on her curvy hips. "I'm not playing anything, Orlando. I'm here to make sure you walk again."

I dropped the smirk and gave her the respect she deserved. Because underneath it all, she was my champion. I needed that more than anything. Having lived an easy life, I felt helpless. At least around Harriet I could vent the weak, edgy douche I'd become. Despite her occasional one-finger salute, she seemed to take me in all my shades of shithead.

I dropped the joker's smirk. "You know, I couldn't do this with anyone else?"

"You're doing great." She smiled. "When you can be bothered, that is." She reverted to her bossy tone, which always stirred my dick. "Would you like some coffee and pie?"

"Sure," I said.

I held her gaze, and as always, looking confused, she'd bite her lip and turn away sharply.

Carrying a plate with a slice of pie and a cup in the other hand, Harriet set it down on the table by my side.

"Where's yours?" I asked.

"I don't feel like it."

"Have some pie with me. I insist."

She tilted her head, about to challenge me, when her phone rang. "I need to take this."

As I swallowed a spoonful of pie, I looked at my guitar, upright on its stand. I was expecting Miles to arrive. We were working on a few original tunes, which had reignited my interest in music again.

It used to be difficult not to play music. Now, I struggled to pick it up. But that was slowly changing thanks to Harriet, who was always encouraging me to play.

Harriet returned. "Sorry about that."

"Your boyfriend?" I grinned.

Harriet laughed. "I don't have one of those."

I restrained from telling her I thought the guys of LA must have been blind or gay.

3

HARRIET

Remaining deadpan to Orlando's constant flirting tested my inner tart.

Why did he have to be so hot with that messy dark hair, looking like he'd been fucking all night?

My carefully thought-out responses had me balancing on a tightrope. It didn't take much for Orlando's playfulness to fade and his glum face to return.

Showering him was the most challenging part of my job. He'd get an erection when I dried him. I tried not to look. But we had a history. Just that one night in Venice. He'd forgotten. But my body memorized every delicious inch.

I'd even caught Orlando jerking off. I salivated as he fisted his big dick. We both pretended we didn't see. It was a game. A sexy little game.

I had it bad. That's why I went to great lengths to get the job at the hospital in the first place.

My obsession for Orlando Thornhill had led me to do something regrettable. My gut turned into stone just thinking about how I'd gotten down on my knees at that interview.

"That was my mother," I said. "I have to pick up Ava and drive her to Miranda's. Do you mind if I leave soon? I'll be back for our exercise session later."

"You go," he said.

Just as I passed him, he grabbed my hand. "I couldn't do this without you, Harry. You know that, don't you?" A serious glint touched his eyes.

A shiver ran through me. After a few drinks, Orlando opened up one night and admitted that while lying in hospital unable to move, he kept thinking of ways to end his life.

"I'm here. Always." I smiled tightly. "In any case, your mobility's improving. It's only been three months. I think that you're on track to make a full recovery. I believe it's inflammation and not permanent damage."

He shrugged. "Who knows? I don't want to get my hopes up."

I squeezed his shoulder.

"So, a few drinks tonight, yeah?" he asked. His boyish glow had returned.

Accustomed to his abrupt mood swings, I unclenched my palms. I'd learned to ride his changes like a surfer does a choppy wave.

"Sure," I said. "I'll pick up a six-pack."

"No need. Mary always stocks the fridge. Without me even having to ask." He chuckled.

Orlando's occasional bout of heavy drinking was another habit I turned a blind eye to. He was that unusual drinker who could drink a lot without becoming an asshole. If anything, beer made him calmer. Something he put down to Irish genes.

I grabbed my bag. "Catch you soon."

Drawing in the pleasant salty air, I headed to my old car, which looked like a hobo at a lavish ball, parked next to a collection of luxury vehicles—an impressive fleet of colorful vintages and slick electric cars.

After battling the afternoon rush, I finally arrived at my parent's home and found my mother teaching Ava how to knit of all things.

Fuzzy warmth flushed through me as I observed my daughter's little fingers looping the wool over the needle. That was me once—an innocent little girl knitting scarves and beanies.

Ava scampered over and showed me her knitting, which had dropped the odd stitch and was uneven but still miraculous for such little hands.

"That's fantastic, sweetie," I said, looking up at my father, who smiled at me as he lounged back, bingeing on episodes of *National Geographic*.

I pecked him on the cheek. "Hey, Dad."

"You've gone pink this week, I see," he said, chuckling. He thought my hair choices were creative.

My mom popped her knitting down and rose. "She's got beautiful hair, and she goes and gets that trailer-trash look."

I rolled my eyes. I'd heard it all before. "Stop being a snob, Mom."

Ignoring my swipe, she asked, "Has your sister mentioned a wedding ceremony? We haven't even met him yet. Can you believe her eloping? It's something you might have done, but not Miranda. She was always the sensible one."

I released a frustrated breath. As usual, she compared me with my sister, with me being the disappointment. But I refused to sink to petty resentment. Miranda had always supported me. It was my mother I was sore at.

"That's so last century, Mom. Nobody elopes anymore. Speaking of last century, what's with the knitting? I haven't seen you do that since Ava was a baby."

She shrugged. "I found a whole lot of wool while cleaning out the cupboards and thought it would be nice to teach Ava. She enjoyed it. It's a useful skill. You used to. Remember?"

I nodded. It was a favorite pastime along with sewing. Until teen hormones kicked in, and I swapped my hobbies for boys.

I regarded Ava, who was showing my father a backbend. If only she'd remain innocent forever. And she was so beautiful. Even though good looks opened doors, it also got girls into trouble.

"Come into the kitchen, while I make coffee. I want to hear about Miranda's new husband."

"You're looking skinnier, sweetheart," my father said as I passed him.

"I've been busy working, I suppose." I smiled at him. My father, unlike my mom was a man of few words. He had a calming influence, and I loved him madly for his unconditional support, especially around my mother's endless bickering born out of her unrealistic expectations.

I joined my mother in the kitchen. "I don't have much time. I've got to pack. We're moving into Malibu."

She looked up at me while pouring water into a cup. "That's where your sister has moved."

I nodded. "She's married a billionaire."

"One that we haven't met," she added.

"Miranda mentioned you're having dinner tonight," I said. "You'll meet Lachlan, then. He's nice. And very good looking."

She stopped what she was doing. "And that matters, I suppose."

"Well, Dad wasn't exactly ugly," I said, in response to her sarcasm.

"Hey," my father called out. "I can hear. Be nice."

My mother rolled her eyes. "So, you're moving there, too?"

"It's for work. I'm caring for Orlando Thornhill."

She studied me for a moment. "You're not together, are you?"

I took a deep breath and did my utmost to look shocked. Perceptive to the point of intrusiveness, my mother could've read tarot cards, if she weren't such a skeptic.

I shook my head. "That would get me into trouble. I'm his nurse."

"And Ava?" she asked, passing me a cup of coffee.

"I'm moving into a cottage that's bigger than my condo."

Ava came running into the kitchen. I put my arm around her. "Did you hear that, we're moving to Malibu. Right on the beach. Next door to Aunty Andie."

"And Manuel," she said excitedly.

"Manuel's her dance partner," I related back to mother.

"Yes. I've heard about him. What about her school?" she asked.

Ava reached up to the plate of cookies and looked at me and my mother before taking one. I nodded. Overly preoccupied with curiosity, my mother overlooked my daughter's sweet tooth for once.

I chomped on a chocolate cookie and swallowed it before answering. "Miranda and me will take turns driving her to school."

"The schools around Malibu would probably be of better quality."

"I don't know how long I'll be there. It might only be three months or less or more." I looked down at my hands. Everything was so uncertain. I felt jumpy about my attachment to my patient, reminding myself repeatedly I was there to care for him and not fall in love.

"As long as she's not too tired from all that travelling. I hope you'll find time to visit us."

"Of course. Anyway, I'm sure Miranda will invite you to stay."

"Mm… I like the sea. But we're ordinary people. We'd look strange there."

I laughed. "Oh, Mom, you overthink everything. The Thornhills are good, down-to-earth people. And they're also a very bright and talented lot. Aidan and Orlando are both amazing musicians. Clarissa's an art expert. Her father Julian used to lecture in literature."

She nodded, looking impressed for a change. "What about Miranda's new husband? I want to hear about him."

I looked at the clock. "I've got to go." I gulped down my coffee. "He's a great guy. You'll like him."

"But does he read? Is he intelligent?"

"He's a good person. That's all that counts."

My father joined us and nodded. "Harry's right, Jane."

"Now, who asked you, Mike?"

He looked at me and smiled.

"I've really got to go," I said.

Following me around as I gathered Ava's belongings, my mother chatted away about all kinds of things and after kissing her on the cheek and saluting my dad, we left.

4

ORLANDO

Allegra flicked pages of her latest assignment. She'd chosen to study fashion design, taking after our mother, who was also a gifted artist.

"These are great," I said, proud of my sister's talent and focus.

"Thanks. Mom and Dad are really pleased. I'm going to submit them for fashion week."

"Oh… you mean to have your clothes in a parade?" I asked.

She nodded. "I've started whipping up some samples."

"I didn't realize you could sew," I said.

"I'm taking lessons. It's fun." She smiled sweetly.

Allegra not only inherited our mother's love of clothes and drawing, but she possessed the same gentle nature.

We were nothing alike in looks or personality. But unlike some siblings, we never fought. She'd always let me lead the way — from the design of our cubby house to the naming of our pets and who to invite to our parties.

According to my dad, I took after his father, who apparently was wild in his younger days.

Allegra touched my hand. "How are you really doing, Ollie?"

I shrugged. "Some days I'm okay; others not so good."

She smiled sadly. "Harriet seems really optimistic about your recovery."

Facing the courtyard, we sat on the porch, under a shady old willow.

A bluebird landed on the table. "Look at that sweet creature," sang Allegra, reminding me of when she was young. I found it difficult to think of Allegra as a grown-up. She had an amusing, childish side to her. As a ridiculous giggler, she always dragged me in. I'd often end up holding my belly in stitches. For no reason at all.

She went inside, and returned with seed, and refilled the bowl held up by a marbled goddess.

"Thanks for doing that," I said. I loved watching birds soar in the sky. Flying was something I'd often fantasized about.

Now, all I could dream of was walking again. A normal bodily function I once took for granted by thrashing myself about as though I was made of steel.

"Dad mentioned that you're working on some music with Miles."

I nodded. "He's due any minute." Footsteps sounded and assuming it was him, I turned to look. Instead, I saw Harriet and her daughter heading toward us.

The bubbly little blonde girl ran over to us and waved.

"Hey," Allegra said, smiling.

"Hello. I'm Ava."

"Pleased to meet you, I'm Allegra."

Harriet placed her luggage down and joined us. "Hey there."

Allegra kissed my nurse on the cheek. "You're doing such a great job with Ollie."

"It's nothing, really. He's doing all the work. I'm just bossy." Harriet looked at me and pulled a face.

I chuckled. "She is really bossy."

"He does need to be told sometimes. Oh, brother of mine," she said, rising. "I best be going."

"Miles will be here in a minute. In fact, here he is." I pointed toward our neighbor as he stepped into the courtyard.

My sister's cheeks reddened which made me wonder if they'd already started dating. By the way he gave her his undivided attention, and how they were always lost in their own world when together, Miles's crush wasn't a secret. It was Allegra who kept things close to her chest.

Carrying his portable keyboard, Miles joined us on the porch. He looked at Allegra and smiled awkwardly, before saluting everyone else.

Harriet turned to me. "We might just move in and get set up. Is there anything you need?"

"No. But Mom asked me to invite you and Ava to dinner."

She smiled. "As long as we're not intruding,"

"No way. There's always heaps of food. You should stay, too, Miles."

"Yeah. Great." He looked at Allegra and she smiled back.

"I've got to go." Allegra patted my arm and left.

After Harriet and Ava headed off, I turned to Miles and said, "Let's go and play some music."

He offered to push me, and I shook my head. "I'm good. My arms are getting really strong doing this."

"They look it, dude. They're huge."

I had to laugh at that exaggeration. But it felt good to know one part of my body was strong and capable.

We'd been practicing a new tune for an hour when Harriet knocked on the door.

"Come in," I said, setting my guitar down. "You don't have to knock, you know."

She'd changed into a pretty floral dress, which was unusual for her, since she normally wore jeans. I liked her in anything. The fewer clothes, the better.

Her legs were as shapely as the rest of her, and I felt a sudden twitch in my groin. "You're looking all summery," I said.

"I just took Ava for a walk down to the beach. She's outside tossing a ball to the dog."

"Hendrix will go all day," I said, chuckling. That was me as a kid, watching my dog fly through the air, catching the ball in his mouth.

"Hey, that sounded great," she said.

"Thanks, we're just mucking around." I looked over at Miles covering his keyboard. "You should keep that here. It saves you dragging it over. Unless you're using it at home."

He shook his head. "I've got the electric Rhodes in my room, and the grand in the living room."

"Is it time for a beer?" I asked.

"It's six o'clock," Miles said. "I could use one." He headed to the kitchen. "Do you want one, Harriet?"

"Why not," she said. "It's Friday." She looked at me and smiled.

Harriet's daughter turned and finished her little performance with her arms in the air, and everyone clapped.

The table was filled with dinner guests, and my mom, who loved having the family together, was in her element. With lots of interesting stories to tell, my grandfather Julian had just returned from England with my Aunt Greta.

"Your daughter's so talented," my mom said to Harriet. "Is she just studying Spanish?"

"Ballet, too," Harriet replied.

It took a lot of guts to bring up a child alone. And Ava was a great kid. She seemed so mature, smart, and well-behaved. Except for her tendency to practice banging her feet everywhere she went. Not that I minded. She amused me.

"Ballet's great for the posture," my mother continued. "I studied it for a while. My grandmother was Spanish. I would've loved to have done flamenco."

"You've got the looks for it," Harriet said.

My dad looked at my mom with a warm glow in his eyes. They were in love, which was kind of icky and sweet. I couldn't imagine my life without them being together. Having family around meant the world to me.

One day, I hoped for my own family.

But would that be possible now that I was an invalid?

I could have sex. I wanted to have sex. Especially with my nurse.

But what about shooting hoops with my kid, or even teaching them to surf?

I still craved the sea. Even though she'd sucked me under and wanted to do away with me, I still missed the buzz of surfing.

"Ava, come and sit down," Harriet said. She looked up at my parents. "I'm sorry, she's really obsessed and never stops practicing. I'll make sure she doesn't disturb anyone. Manuel's her dance partner, so I'll encourage her to practice at Lachlan and Miranda's."

"We don't mind. We love it. We're used to it around here." My mother looked at my dad and smiled.

Harriet looked puzzled, and I said, "Dad has his occasional Hendrix moment and lets it rip. Especially since picking up Hendrix's famous Marshall amp."

"It was a Fender Twin Reverb," my dad corrected me.

"The house almost shakes. But we like it." My mom regarded him with a sparkle in her eyes.

"Oh… the electric guitar," Harriet said. "I thought you were talking about Hendrix the dog."

"He's so cute," Ava said.

Everyone laughed. My father smiled the brightest. I could see he loved having a kid around, and he always used to clown around with us when we were little.

"Creativity is well and truly invited here," he said. "Ava can be as noisy as she likes. It's inspiring. I love flamenco guitar."

I nodded. "It's hot and seriously complex. The rhythms are, at least."

"I believe you're working on some tunes," my father asked, shifting his focus to Miles.

"Kind of folksy jazz numbers, I suppose," Miles said in his humble fashion.

Mature for his age, Miles might have come across as the silent type, but he had depth and tons of talent. He was a great match for my sister, despite him being younger. I would have hated Allegra dating guys like my former partying pals. Their crappy attitudes toward women made me so sick I'd stopped seeing them. Which hadn't been difficult since we hadn't spoken since my accident.

"Is there any singing?" my mom asked.

"No. But we've been thinking about it. Ollie's written some cool lyrics." Miles glanced at me.

"You can sing, Ollie," Allegra said.

"He's got a great voice," my father added.

"Mm... I don't know." I shrugged. "I've never had a go at lyrics before. I'm enjoying the process."

"Why don't you play something?" my grandfather asked.

Everyone encouraged us to perform. And the next thing I knew, my amp was carried into the living room next to the piano, where my mother arranged for dessert to be served.

While Miles jumped onto the piano that Allegra and I used to practice on, I glanced over at Harriet, who returned a smile.

Having not performed for a while, I enjoyed sharing our new material with an audience. Even if it was only family. I could have played a ukulele while balancing a ball on my nose, and they still would have considered me a prodigy.

There was no doubt my love of performing came from my grandfather, who started playing gigs when he was my age, and was famous for endless partying and women.

Now, I wouldn't even be able to fuck on the beach or anywhere else for that matter.

It wasn't until Harriet became my nurse and sponged me down in hospital, that my dick moved for the first time after the accident. Her scent and breast touching my arm made my heart pound.

We performed four of our tunes, and as I placed my guitar in its case, rapturous applause filled the room.

"They're so funky and toe-tapping. You've got a really nice groove going there," my dad said.

My mother hugged me and Miles. "You're both so talented."

I smiled. I'd had a great night. For the first time since the accident, I almost felt like myself again.

"Creativity will make you well again," said my grandfather, patting my shoulder.

After we all said our goodbyes, I followed Harriet to her new home, which was next door to mine. I couldn't wheel into her cottage because there was no ramp, so I remained at the bottom of her porch as she stood in the moonlight looking sexy.

"Ava's exhausted," she said. "Too much excitement. And she's got dance class tomorrow. I'm glad Miranda's offered to drive them."

"Then if you don't have to rush off in the morning, you can come back for a drink."

My eyes feasted on her. Wearing her hair down and with those large, sultry dark eyes, Harriet was hot. I loved the way her lips parted slightly when I stumped her. Like that moment. I'm sure she read my invitation as me hitting on her.

"I guess I could have one," she said. "We're close. Next door."

"Great. See you in a minute," I said. "Don't take too long. I might get lonely."

Her mouth curled at one end, and she tilted her head as she often did whenever I flirted with her.

5

HARRIET

After tucking Ava into bed, I took a quick tour of our new temporary home before heading over to Orlando's for a drink.

Our comfort wasn't spared. There were fresh cotton sheets on the beds, and the rooms smelled of lavender.

The spacious living room, with its modern furnishings, original art, and large TV screen on the wall, made the space more luxury condo than cottage.

I poked my head into the well-stocked fridge and couldn't believe how considerate and generous the Thornhills were. A pang of guilt swept through me for flirting with their son.

Being a hot night, I changed into a tank top and shorts, then locked the screen door so I could listen out for Ava. Orlando's cottage was directly next door, and the entrance to that high-walled estate was like Fort Knox. And then there was Hendrix, who'd taken up camp on our porch. That handsome dog had taken a liking to Ava in what had become an instant mutual love affair. When he followed at our heels, Aidan reassured me it was okay for Hendrix to hang out with us.

I knocked on the Orlando's door.

"Come in if you're naked," he said.

"Then I better not enter." I giggled.

Orlando wheeled to the door and opened it for me. He seemed to insist on doing everything himself, and I respected that.

Clarissa had been responsible for decking out the cottage with Orlando's belongings and personality. I enjoyed being in his creative space, where sheet music, instruments, and an assortment of eye-catching record sleeves lay about. When Orlando wasn't practicing, he'd have music coming from his turntable. I'd learned a lot about music and had developed a fondness for jazz.

"We should hear, shouldn't we, if Ava calls out?" I asked, standing at the door.

"Sure. And there's nothing to worry about, Hendrix is a great watchdog." Orlando lowered the needle onto a record. "The only unwanted visitors are of the furry variety, and even then, Hendrix would pounce."

I smiled in response to his chuckle as I settled down on the sofa. "I just can't believe how generous your parents are. The cottage is so nice. There's food in the fridge. And the beds are made."

He sniffed. "Welcome to billionaire comfort."

I shook my head. "It's surreal. You really have a great life."

His face went a little darker.

I took a deep breath. "I'm sorry... I."

"Don't," he said, wheeling out into the kitchen. "Beer?"

I followed him and instead of offering to help, as my instincts dictated, I held back.

When he opened the fridge, I noticed the bottles were positioned on the top shelf and out of his reach.

I offered to get them, but he shook his head. "Don't." He lifted himself off his chair. His legs trembled.

My heart gripped. I wanted to help.

Wearing a determined frown, he stretched up and grabbed the bottle when it slipped from his hand and shattered. Smashing glass echoed off the tiled floor, and my nerves jumped with the ear-splitting crash.

I bent down to help when he yelled, "Don't!"

He tried again. "Don't watch me," he demanded.

I held my breath and turned away. Sweat trickled between my shoulder blades.

From the side of my eyes, I spied him clutching hold of a bottle this time, while lowering himself with a tremor into his chair.

Swallowing the painful lump in my throat, where angry words banked up, doused in pity, I left the kitchen and sat on the sofa with my head in my hands. Working in rehab among desperate drug addicts hadn't prepared me for this. It was my fault. If I weren't so deeply involved, I would have reverted to my take-no-bullshit approach. I needed to be tough again, not this crumbling mess that I'd become.

My head told me to leave him alone, but that would have inflamed the situation. Orlando was used to getting what he wanted. Such snooty behavior I normally wouldn't have tolerated, but I'd turned into putty around him.

He rolled back in with two bottles on his lap. Even that looked tenuous; the slightest shift and they would've tumbled.

Orlando passed one to me.

"Thanks," I said, removing it from his hand. As our fingers touched and electricity sparked through me. He looked into my eyes, as though he felt it, too.

I gripped my drink in tense silence. After a few calming sips, I asked, "Have I've done something to piss you off?"

"It's not you. It's me and these fucking useless legs."

I rose from the couch to clean the broken glass in the kitchen.

"Where are you going?" he asked.

"I'm just going to clear the mess in the kitchen."

"Don't," he said abrasively.

"But you could cut yourself."

His spine-chilling laugh thickened the air. "You mean my tires being slashed?"

I rose. "I can't handle you when you're like this."

He lifted his hand. "Stay."

I headed to the door.

"I'm paying you to do as I say."

My eyebrows contracted sharply. "What?"

"You heard me. Sit," he said, pointing to the couch.

"You can't talk to me like that," I shot back and, fueled by defiance, returned to the kitchen.

He wheeled in. "I told you to leave that alone. You're not my fucking cleaner."

Ignoring him, I remained on my hands and knees, carefully picking up the larger pieces of glass.

He rolled next to me and grabbed my arm. "Stop."

Our eyes locked. His angry, dark stare also showed frustration and pain.

I returned to my task with steely determination until every bit of glass was cleared.

"It's done." I wiped my hands. "I'm leaving. You can stew alone in your own shit."

"You can't talk to me like that."

Ignoring him, I headed into the living room and grabbed my bag.

"I said, you can't go." He followed me to the door.

As his gaze held me captive, I recognized a fragile glint. A cry for help.

Orlando was young, but right then, shadowed by the lamp, he looked older, as though a demon had visited him.

He took my hand and squeezed it hard. It should have hurt, but I understood his need for a punching bag. At the rehab clinic, I'd experienced my fair share of angst. The more I tried to ignore drug-addicted patients, the louder they screamed out of some frenzied need to share their despair.

I took a deep breath and remained at the door. One leg in, one leg out.

"Stay," he pleaded. His eyes softened.

I returned to the sofa and sat down.

Gripped by tension, we drank in silence.

Despite eyeing my hands, I felt his burning gaze.

"Why are you looking at me?" I asked at last.

"Because you're nice to look at. You're sexy."

I studied him with a question.

"Do you realize you were the last woman I fucked?" He cocked his head slightly as though trying to read my mind.

I sat up. "But that was what a week or so before your accident."

"It was three weeks before my accident." He kept staring into my eyes.

My body trembled within. I had to shift away from his penetrating gaze, so I rose and picked up an album cover of a guitarist in full flight off the floor.

"Why?" I finally asked.

"Why, what?"

"Why are you telling me this?" I asked.

"Because I want you to know I'm not as immature as you think."

"I never thought you were."

He sipped his beer and continued looking at me. "I haven't touched a woman's body since yours."

"And I haven't been with anyone since you, either."

I gulped back my beer, still processing his earlier admission. "Why didn't you ring me?"

He shrugged. "I don't know. I wanted to." His gaze burned into mine and then wandered down my body. I could almost feel him touching me.

"Why act as if you didn't know me then?" I asked the question that'd been bugging me since becoming his nurse.

"I recognized you when you turned up at the hospital. You're not the type of girl a guy easily forgets, Harry." He remained deadpan. "I felt ashamed. You seeing me crippled like that. It hurt to remember the good times. And you *were* a good time."

"I'm still here," I said. Was I offering myself to him?

"Don't I know it."

"Would you prefer I left?" I asked.

"No fucking way." His stare penetrated deeply. "You get me."

I looked up at him, and our eyes held, swimming in each other's emotional turbulence. "You're more attractive than most guys who can walk," I admitted.

He looked down at his feet and stretched his leg out.

"You're getting more mobility. You're doing great," I said.

His face darkened again. "Then why do I feel like such fucking shit?"

I let out a frustrated sigh. More at myself for bringing up his body. "I don't know what to say."

"Then don't. Just fucking sit there and turn me on."

"What?" I dropped my jaw.

"Just that." He finished his beer, rolled over to the turntable and flipped the album over.

Soothing jazz guitar did little to clear the sudden rush of sexual tension.

"You want me to do what?" I asked.

"I want to see you naked."

I gulped. He undid his zipper. And even though I'd seen his dick, this time my body burned. I was no longer his nurse.

"I'm sick of playing with myself. I don't want just anyone's mouth on my dick."

I also didn't want anyone's mouth on his dick.

"Take off that top." He gestured. "At least let me look at your tits."

His bossy tone inflamed me. I could hardly breathe. I stood up. "You can't demand that of me."

He pointed at the couch. "Sit."

"No, I fucking won't." Sexual hunger fired me up. It hurt not to scream out of frustration. If I weren't his nurse, I would have been naked by now.

I charged to the door. I had to, before doing something I'd regret. I fought to quash a sudden raging appetite to pleasure him. Had we been anywhere but his family's home, and I weren't paid handsomely to care for him, I would have dropped to my knees with his dick deep in my throat.

"Don't go," he said. "I'm sorry for being out of line."

I sat down again and took a steadying breath. "Look Orlando, I'm being paid to heal you. Look after you."

"Trust me. Seeing you naked and you touching my dick would be very healing." He smirked and then went serious again. "I remember everything about you, Harry. The way you felt when I was inside of you. And how your soft tits moved. And how fucking hot you are all over. And how you came in my mouth and made me want to blow just from that."

I gulped tightly. I'd been with much older men and none had spoken so openly to me. His words stroked my swollen clit.

Sipping on my beer, I felt my nipples tighten. I knew he'd noticed because his gaze wandered down to my chest and returned to my face, searing into me.

What was I to do? I was on fire.

My inner pleasure-seeker took control. I removed my tank top. *What harm could it do?* This was between us. And I was dripping wet and equally hungry.

"You've got such gorgeous tits," he said, his voice hoarse. "Take off the bra."

Unclasping my bra, I let it fall to the ground. I sat there topless. My nipples hard and crying for his lips.

He ran his tongue over his mouth, and he crooked his finger.

Each step brought me closer to crossing that line.

6

ORLANDO

I patted my thighs. "Sit on my lap." I couldn't think, let alone talk, seeing her tits with those rosy, and erect nipples.

"I might hurt you," she said.

"Just get here."

"You're being all bossy again," she said, lowering herself onto my thighs.

Turning to face me, she ran her tongue over her lips.

To feel a woman again had become a desperate need. An adventure. And not just any woman, but Harriet. I could be myself around her. She accepted me even in my useless state.

Our tentative lips touched as though it was our first, which wasn't the case. We'd both had our share of kisses.

My heart raced. I'd been dying to feel her lips, from the moment Harriet turned up as my nurse, even after pretending I didn't know her.

How could anyone forget Harriet? She was hot. And even though I'd hated her, along with everyone, including me, who I hated the most, whenever she bent down to take my temperature, my dick thickened.

Soft and sweet, that kiss was like a journey of discovery.

I'd forgotten how a mouth could be so erotic.

As our tongues tangled, I caressed and fondled her breasts.

"You've got beautiful tits. Just the right size. Not too big or too small," I said, sucking on her beaded nipples.

"They're not very big," she said in a breathy voice.

"They're big enough. I don't like huge tits. Yours are perfect." I kept caressing them as though acquainting myself with them more.

"I'm thinking of having them enlarged."

I shook my head. "You're crazy. Why would you do that?"

She shrugged. "I thought all men liked big tits."

"No way. That's porno shit. Forget it. And they're soft and really sexy."

She stood up and lowered her shorts.

"Turn around, let me see that perfect ass," I said, breathing so heavily I could barely talk.

Harriet giggled as she turned while I ogled her curvy butt, poking out of her thong.

I pulled out my cock and jerked at it. "Remove your panties and spread your legs."

She sat opposite me and opened her legs wide.

I sighed. Seeing her glistening pink slit all wide and ready did things to me I had never felt before. By now, my former able self would have been in there, pounding hard and fast.

Harriet's lips parted as she played with her clit while her smoldering gaze drugged me. She looked beautiful when aroused.

"I want to watch you come," I said, fisting my dick.

She rose from the couch and stood before me, lowering onto her knees. Her face landed on my lap and she wrapped her luscious mouth around my erection.

I dropped my head back. "Ah…"

She went in deep, too. Real deep. And her tongue, and the gentle scraping of teeth that should have hurt, made me see stars.

Her fleshy mouth moved up and down, devouring my dick as though it was a delicious treat.

I would have paid a fortune for that image of Harriet's large eyes gazing up at me, while her full lips wrapped around my inflamed dick.

Her tongue lashed my shaft while sucking me deep to her throat. She was an expert. As she moved faster and faster, in and out, my head felt like it would explode. The friction. The blood rush beat any drug I'd ever tried.

It was the best blowjob I'd ever had. And I'd had my fair share.

"I'm going to come." I groaned.

Clinging tightly to my dick, she licked, sucked and teased while sliding her lips up and down my length.

A hot rush swept through me and grunting, I shot deeply into her. It seemed to flow out in torrents. I'd been jerking off daily, but that paled compared to Harriet sucking me off.

When my senses returned, I shook my head. "Holy fuck. That was the blowjob of the fucking century." I ran my finger over her swollen red lips. "You've got a very sexy mouth."

"I'm glad to be of service," she said, standing up and rubbing her knees.

Although she'd delivered it with a cheeky grin, that comment jarred. I hated her thinking this was now part of our arrangement, despite my body craving for more of her.

7

HARRIET

"Wake up, Mommy." Ava shook me. Dreaming of nestling in Orlando's arms, I'd been in such a deep sleep I woke disorientated, taking me a moment to recognize my new bedroom.

I rubbed my eyes. "What time is it?" When I saw it was nine o'clock, I sprung up. "Oh… I slept in." I looked at my daughter. "Sorry, sweetie. Have you got your stuff together for class?"

She nodded.

"You'll need breakfast," I said, jumping out of bed. A slight jaw ache confirmed that I hadn't dreamt of blowing Orlando. It had actually happened. His was the biggest dick I'd ever had in my mouth. The thought made my pussy throb.

While searching for clothes, I realized I hadn't even unpacked properly. Fuzzy-headed, all I could think of was that blow job.

As I gazed off into the distance, my body became heavy. We'd crossed that line, and now what? Would I look at him as a nurse, or as someone obsessed. After all, he'd been my obsession from the word go. What did that make me?

Suddenly, the lines blurred, considering how I'd gotten that job in the first place.

I took a deep breath and blew out slowly to regain my focus.

"I've already had some cereal." Ava tugged at my hand, snapping me out of my daze.

For a five-year-old, she really had her act together. Despite that, I still hated myself for being so caught up in Orlando to overlook my maternal duties.

"You're a clever girl."

"I need to go, Mommy," she said, always serious and driven when it came to dance classes.

I texted Miranda to tell her we were on our way.

Fifteen minutes later, I stood at the entrance of my sister's palatial home.

She answered all bright-eyed and bubbly. "Hey. I was about to call."

"Sorry. I had a big night." I leaned over and whispered. "I need to talk to you. Can we catch up later? Since you're my neighbor." I chuckled at the insanity of us living in such billionaire luxury.

"I should be back later. I'll text you and drop in. Your patient won't mind?" she asked.

"It's Saturday. In any case, he's made it quite clear I can live a normal life. Whatever that means." I knew what it meant. Me being there at his beck and call seven days a week. I didn't mind.

But would that now include me on my knees sucking his dick? Or him having me finger myself?

Ava tugged at my blouse. "Mommy, we need to go."

I smiled. "She's obsessed. Saturday's her day. All-day classes. Manuel's going, I take it?"

"Oh god, yeah. He's just as into it."

I kissed Ava and Miranda and strolled back to my new home.

When I reached the cottage, I spied Orlando on the porch reading, and headed over to speak to him.

"Hey. Sorry, I didn't drop in earlier. Is everything okay?" I asked.

"Why wouldn't it be?" he asked, peering up from his magazine.

I swallowed tightly. "I just dropped Ava off at Miranda's. I thought you'd still be in bed."

"I woke up early," he said. His face barely moving.

I didn't expect him to hug and kiss me, but still a smile wouldn't have hurt.

"I might grab a coffee and something to eat. Can I get you something?" I asked.

"A muffin. They've just been baked."

I nodded. "Coming right up. I'll be back."

I stepped into the main house and headed for the kitchen. Although Clarissa had said I was welcomed anytime, it still felt strange being there.

Mary, the maid who might have been in her midthirties, moved about the large space decked with stainless steel benchtops, resembling an industrial kitchen.

An aroma of freshly baked sweets traveled through me, making my stomach rumble.

"Hey, Mary, do you mind if I take a couple?" I pointed at the tray of muffins.

"I was about to pop over with some. You've saved me a trip."

I smiled. "Thanks for stocking up our fridge and cupboards with food."

"Clarissa instructed me to make sure you had everything."

"They're so generous," I said.

"That they are. They like how you've helped with Ollie. You've made a difference. I can see it."

"I hope I can get him there. He gets in these moods."

"Tell me about it." She grimaced. "He used to be so easygoing and happy all the time. It's like he's become someone else. But then, I do understand. Poor thing. He's been through hell."

I nodded pensively. "Have you worked here long?"

"About fifteen years. I started here straight out of college and never left."

"You live here, too?" I asked.

"Yeah. It's a great setup. And I like a quiet life." She smiled shyly.

"If you ever want to drop in for a chat, you know where to find me."

"I'd love that. I often chat with Allegra. She's so nice."

"I best be getting back to Orlando. He can get a little impatient." I shook my head at his petulance. In fact, sometimes I thought he was a complete asshole. But then, were I in his place, I'd be the same.

When I returned, I found Orlando strumming his guitar, and set down a plate by his side.

"We'll need to do some exercises after breakfast," I said, trying to sound as normal as possible.

"I've already done some."

I scanned his face. That was new. He normally needed a push to exercise. "How did you go?"

He headed over to the hallway where exercise bars were installed.

Raising himself off his chair, he stood up. My heart skipped a beat as he remained upright, holding onto the bar.

The determination and strain in his face as though he'd planned to conquer a major milestone stirred emotion. I had to bite my lip.

"Oh, my god. That's the longest you've stood."

He remained pitched against the bar. When his legs wobbled, I went to take his arm, but he shook his head. "No, let me do it." He lowered himself into his chair. His bulging muscles straining.

"Your arms are so strong," I said.

He looked up at me, and a corner of his mouth curled up.

"This afternoon, why don't we go to rehab gym. I think you're ready to be harnessed."

Orlando cast me a puzzled smirk. "Harnessed? Like S&M?"

I tilted my head and grinned. "Well, not quite."

"Pity. You'd look hot with nipple rings and a chocker around that long, slender neck."

My nipples tightened and his eyes radared in.

"In your dreams," I returned, tilting my head.

He took my hand. His smiling eyes turned sultry, and a burning ache between my legs started up again.

A knock came to the door, making me jump. I jerked my hand away and went to answer it.

As Aidan stood before me, I prayed he wouldn't notice the streak of guilt flushing my cheeks.

"Hey, Dad." Orlando wheeled down the hallway.

Aidan stepped into the living room and popped a magazine on the table. "I thought I'd drop in the latest *Mojo*."

"Would you like a juice or something?" I asked.

"No, thanks. I'm off to an auction." He grinned. "I'm a collector of old guitars."

"He's got a museum up there," Orlando said. A sad smile touched his lips, and I noticed a look of sympathy from Aidan, who generally kept a brave face. Clarissa was the one that often turned away with a tear on her cheek.

"We're putting a lift in the house. You'll be able to come up and visit your grandfather, too."

Orlando looked at me. "Julian's got this incredible library. He's always coming down to read for me." He chuckled.

"That's a great idea about putting in a lift," I said to Aidan. "But I think Orlando's really close."

Aidan studied me with an intense frown. "What do you mean?"

"Come on, Harry, don't fill my dad with false hope."

"Show your dad what you just showed me. Please." I gave Orlando an encouraging nod.

We followed him back to his practice bar. Rubbing his hands, he lifted himself off the chair and stood up. His legs didn't shake as much either.

I shook my head in disbelief and looked at Aidan, who said, "Can I call your mother? That's great, son."

Orlando smiled. He'd recognized a turning point. "Sure. As long as she promises not to cry." He rolled his eyes and sat in his chair again.

I patted his arm. "That was awesome. It's the strongest you've been. Surely, you felt that?"

He shrugged, but then I noticed a small smile. It also meant everything to him. But he probably refused to get his hopes up. I got that. I got him.

Clarissa arrived a few minutes later, and Orlando repeated the same miraculous feat.

She hugged him and then me. "That's amazing."

"I'm taking him to rehab gym today. I just made an appointment, and we'll aim for a daily visit. If that suits?" I looked at Orlando.

"Sure. Why not? Less time writing silly songs."

"They're not silly. They're really good," I said. "You need to record them."

"Mm… I might put them down later. I've just got this new software." He looked at his dad, something he always did when talking about music.

Aidan and Clarissa's eyes shone with love and sympathy as they regarded their son.

I walked with them to the courtyard, leaving Orlando with his guitar.

"It's a quantum shift, isn't it?" Clarissa said.

"Something's changed for sure." I tapped my head. "Self-belief helps."

"So, the rehab gym takes it to the next level?" Aidan asked.

I nodded. "They have harnesses and all kinds of equipment to support him, so that subtle muscle groups get worked and strengthened. Even a little bit every day makes a difference. I was always hoping to get him to that level. And now, we've arrived."

"It's been nearly four months," Aidan said.

"That's about right. I think the anti-inflammatories are starting to have an impact. The specialist told me they'll only help if the injury's an inflammation. And seeing his improvement would suggest that."

Clarissa's eyes watered as she took my hand. "Thank you for pushing him. He's improved. I see it in his face. He's happier, especially today. He's almost his old self."

I smiled. Mm… it's amazing what a blowjob does for a man's wellbeing.

Thank god, she couldn't read my thoughts.

Aidan looked at me. "If there's anything you need. Charge everything to this." He handed me a card.

"Oh… You're already supplying me with everything I need. I don't want for anything. But thanks, anyway."

"What about the gym? That obviously comes with a cost. Spare nothing, please."

I didn't take the card. "I'll let you know. He's enrolled as part of the hospital's rehabilitation program. The facilities are there for him seven days a week. It's really not necessary. There aren't really any overheads."

Clarissa hugged me, and they headed back in, holding hands. Talk about great people.

My stomach knotted. What if they found out about my X-rated style of care?

8

ORLANDO

There was no doubt about it, my legs were getting stronger.

Harriet watched on as the physio helped me along on my harness, in what had become a daily activity.

At first, I complained and Harriet—in her take-no-bullshit way—told me it was either that or sit on my ass all my life. That hit hard, but it also made me take one big bite out of a reality sandwich. A plain boring meal, but one that often slapped me back into action.

Despite the harness cutting into my groin, as the days progressed, I liked going there. Mainly because I felt the improvement. It had become easier for me. I also loved the drive along the coast.

"Hell, the surf looks good," I said, staring out the window.

"When you walk again, will you surf?" Harriet asked.

"You really think I'm going to walk?"

"You bet. You must feel it? Each day, you're walking further."

"Yeah. It's hard, though. Fuck. I took it for granted." I rubbed my groin.

She cast me a glance. "It's hurting down there?"

"Down where, nursie?"

"Nursie?" She laughed.

"You've had it in your mouth all week, and you can't say 'dick'?"

She poked her tongue at me, and I smiled.

"To answer to your question, I will surf again."

I contemplated the glistening sapphire streak. Although I'd visited the beach thanks to the new ramp, I missed feeling the salt water on my skin, and my feet squishing on warm, soft sand.

Brought up on the beach all my life, the sea was a part of me. I could never live away from the coast. Cities were fun to party in, but that hit of salty air made me feel alive.

Harriet parked in the driveway next to a delivery truck.

"That's for the party," I said.

"Are you looking forward to it?" she asked, turning off the engine.

"Yeah. I feel good." I touched her hand. "As long as you're there."

She gave me a quivery smile and then climbed out.

She wheeled my chair close, and I held onto the bar and lowered myself into it.

"You're really improving. Your stomach muscles are strong."

I patted my six-pack and grinned. "Maybe we can try the wheel barrow later," I said.

Her eyes ignited with amused curiosity as she looked around to make sure we were alone. Clutching the chair handle, she asked, "Is this okay?"

"Sure. You push. My arms are tired."

"The wheelbarrow?"

"Your torso on the bed. Me behind you. Your legs up on the chair arms."

"That sounds painful." She laughed.

"It's making me hard thinking about it," I said as we moved along the newly constructed ramp that wove all the way to the cottage.

It was late afternoon and, although I was hungry and sweaty after a long session at the gym, all I could think of was Harriet naked.

"I'll go over to the house and see what's cooking if you like," she said.

"No. Stay. There's plenty of snack food here. There'll be a banquet for dinner. It's family first before the guests arrive, which means we'll be eating early."

Harriet nodded.

I grabbed her hand. "I need to feel you."

A frown appeared on her face. I had too many other issues, and having sex with my nurse wasn't one of them.

"I'm worried about your parents finding out," she said.

"So what? I'm a grown-up. We both are."

I grabbed her around the knees and pulled her onto my lap. Her dark eyes had that aroused twinkle that registered straight to my cock.

She placed her arms around my neck, and our lips met. My tongue entered roughly and whipped around her warm mouth. Her moist caressing kiss made my dick turn to steel.

"Let's go into the bedroom. Now," I demanded.

She waved a salute. "Yes, Boss."

I cocked my head and grinned. I loved playing games with my nurse.

Harriet followed me to the bedroom and locked the door.

"Why are you locking it?" I asked.

She shrugged and returned a tight smile. I could see her guilting out over this. But I was too horny to change anything, and I lowered my sweats.

"Do you know what I find disappointing?" I asked, holding my dick.

Getting on her knees while licking her lips, she asked, "What's that?"

"You're not wearing a nurse's uniform. I miss seeing you in it."

She removed her tank top and unclasped her bra. Her naked tits fell into my hands, and I ached to be inside of her.

"You're so predictable." She laughed and licked the top of my cock.

My head fell back. "Mm... how nice."

Her warm, cushiony mouth sent bolts of electricity through me. The pleasure indescribable as she sucked my dick to the point of no return. Better than any drug I'd ever had.

Gasping, I blew into the back of her throat.

After my senses returned, I said, "You give the best head." I fondled her. "And you've also got the nicest set of tits I've ever touched."

"Thanks," she said, wiping her hands. "I'm still thinking of getting that boob job."

I shook my head. "But why?"

Harriet shrugged. "Because it's the thing to do."

"But there's no reason for it. And, trust me, not all men like big tits."

She studied me. "Do you?"

"Not really. I like yours. And they're on the bigger side as it is. Which is fine. They're really nice. I'm looking forward to rubbing my face in them with you bouncing on my cock."

Although she'd been blowing my mind all week with that perfect mouth of hers, I needed more. I had to return the favor. I wanted to taste her. To make her cry out with my dick buried deep, like she did that one night we fucked.

I unzipped her jeans and hooked inside her panties. When she soaked my fingers, I sighed. "I want to taste your pussy."

She rose, removed her jeans and stood before me in a lacy thong.

"God, you're fucking hot." I ran my hand up her silky, naked thigh. "Follow me."

We went into the kitchen, and I pointed at the bench. "Sit there."

Harriet jumped up, and I edged closer.

"When they built this bench, they had us in mind," I said, impressed how my chair slid under. "The proportions are just made for eating pussy."

Harriet laughed. "I'll be sure omit that from my ergonomic report."

"Ha?" My brows gathered.

"It's a recommendation report to make the space easy to navigate."

"Like navigating to the nurse's pretty, juicy cunt?"

She shook her head and laughed. "You're wicked."

"I'm not hearing any complaints," I said, removing her panties.

She wiggled. "This surface is cold. One minute, I need to get a towel."

I feasted on her nakedness as she moved about. "Has anyone ever told you you've got a great ass?"

Harriet placed a towel on the bench before jumping up again. "Um… yeah… you."

I parted her legs and straddled them onto my shoulders. "It was either this or have you sit on my face."

"I'd smother you."

"Mm… nice." I clutched onto her curvy ass and licked her clit like it was chocolate.

I devoured her, lapping her juices as I nibbled and licked her swollen bud. I fucked her with my finger, and she erupted.

Her pelvis thrust forward, and she shuddered in my hands, moaning as her release spurted my tongue.

"Oh," she let out a breath. "I hope I didn't strangle you."

I wiped my lips and tipped my head toward my groin. "Sit on my dick."

Her forehead creased, and she looked at me as though I'd spoken a different language. "I'm clean. I've had a ton of blood tests. You'll have those in your nurse's file."

"I'm on the pill. And I believe you. It's just…"

"No more talking. Please. Just fuck me." I stroked her hand.

"I have to turn my back to you in order to fit in the chair."

"I've got a better idea. Follow me," I said, wheeling myself to the bedroom.

I eased myself off my chair using the bars by the bed and sat on the bed. I patted my thighs, and she lowered onto my hard dick agonizingly slow.

My eyes rolled to back of my head. "Holy fuck. You feel amazing."

"It's a tight fit. You're really big." She groaned.

"You're also pretty tight. Ah…" I battled to speak. The friction was intense and so hot, blood drained from my brain.

Her tits fell into my mouth. Legs or no legs, that position had become my favorite.

Harriet straddled me and moved up and down, using her strong thighs.

"Oh… fuck… I'm in pussy heaven. You're beautiful, Harry."

She moved faster and faster, her breath getting louder.

"I need you to come. I won't last," I said.

She bounced up and down, with me gripping her round hips. It had been a long time and my heart was in my throat, racing like mad.

Her pussy walls spasmed and squeezed the life out of my dick.

Our lips crashed together, and her moans gushed down my throat.

It was the most intense fuck I'd ever had, and the build-up to my release threatened to take me out.

As I blew inside of her, it felt like my head split in half from the sheer force.

Harriet collapsed into my arms and nestled in my neck, panting in unison with me.

"I hope I'm not crushing you," she said.

"No." I fell back onto the bed and took her with me, holding her tight. "It feels nice having you in my arms."

She remained quiet, and I lifted my head.

"Are you okay?" I asked.

"I'm good. I think." She moved out of my arms.

She wiped herself, and then we went to the shower. I sat on my special chair, and she washed my hair. I closed my eyes as she massaged my head and body with bodywash.

"You're so good at this. You've got great hands," I said.

"Glad to be of service," she said.

"You've also got a very expressive pussy, an amazing mouth, and beautiful tits."

"Shame about the face?"

"You're beautiful, Harry."

"What was the first thing you noticed when you met me?" she asked.

Girls loved that question.

"Your eyes."

Her face brightened.

Even though I knew girls liked that answer, with Harriet, it was true.

"My... you're full of compliments today."

"I've always liked you." I took her hand. That sounded so lame, like we'd met at church or something. Not after a gig, drunk and stoned. After fucking all night long, that hookup registered deeply in my DNA, but I kept to that tight to my chest.

"I've always liked you, too." She bit her lip. "And I feel like shit because I haven't bought you a birthday present."

"You've already given me the best present I could've wished for."

Harriet was drying my hair when a knock came at the door.

She scrambled for her clothes. "My hair's wet. Shit."

"Don't worry. You've had a shower before me? Okay?" I grabbed a towel, and she helped wrap it around me. "I'll go."

I laughed at how panicked she'd become. I didn't really care, because from my way of thinking, as an adult, if I wished to fuck my nurse, so what?

I opened door and found my mother there.

"I just dropped in to make sure you're good for six." She looked inside. "Is Harriet here?"

"Um… yeah she's just in the bathroom."

My mother looked at my towel. "She just showered me. We've been at the gym. Harriet did some exercise, too."

There was a gleam in her eyes I recognized well. She sensed something. "So, how was it?"

"It was easier, and I actually walked the whole length of the room."

Her face lit up. "Oh, my god, really?"

"With a harness on, Mom. Let's not get too carried away."

"Okay. I just wanted to make sure Harriet and Ava knew they were invited to the family dinner. Lachlan and Miranda are joining us. With Manuel."

"Great. I haven't caught up with Lachie for a while. I'll let her know." I could tell she had more questions, and said, "Okay, see you at six."

She bent down and kissed me. "Happy birthday, darling."

"Thanks, Mom."

9

HARRIET

Sunning myself on the terrace, I watched Ava and Manuel splashing about in the pool, while Miranda carried her latest health-fad smoothies for us on a tray.

She passed me a glass.

"Wow. How bright. I wouldn't mind my hair this color," I said, pointing at the hot-pink drink.

"That's the pomegranate and goji berries," she said.

I took a tentative sip. "Mm... not bad. Will it also cleanse my sins?"

Miranda laughed. "You'd need more than a health drink to do that."

"Ha ha ha." I shook my head. "I'm an emotional wreck, that's all."

She smiled sadly. "You can always leave?"

I took a deep breath and blew out slowly. "Easier said than done. Where's Lachlan?"

"Surfing."

Ava waved from the pool. "Mommy, watch this." She performed a handstand in the water, followed by a perfect tumble.

"That's great. You've turned into a mermaid," I said.

She jumped out and ran toward me. I grabbed a towel and tossed it over to her.

"You better hurry, sweetie. We've been invited for dinner at six." I looked at Miranda.

"You'll have to get ready, too. It's five."

"I know. Anyway, before you leave, tell me how's it going with the boy?"

"We're..." I cast her a sheepish smile.

"You are? How?"

I had to laugh at her puzzled frown. "It's interesting. Let's just say, I've discovered a few new positions. All seated, of course."

She laughed and then became serious. "Hell, Harriet, this could get you fired. If it were my son, I wouldn't be happy knowing his nurse was fucking him."

I nodded and sighed. "But it's difficult. He's so insistent, and I'm so attracted. Shit." I held my head.

Manuel came out of the water just as Lachlan arrived with a surfboard under his arm.

"Greetings all," he said, looking tanned and content.

He bent down and kissed Miranda. "Wife."

"Husband," returned Miranda.

Grinning like Cheshire cats, they wore marital bliss well.

"Orlando's dinner is at six." Miranda turned to me. "I should go and get ready, too."

"Sure. I'll grab Ava. Thanks for taking her to classes." I rose and gathered my daughter's belongings.

An hour later, we were inside the Thornhills' palatial home, and despite their welcoming down-to-earth ways, I struggled to relax.

In sharp contrast to my silent presence, Ava was in her element. As the consummate social butterfly, my daughter loved being around people. The more the merrier for my chatty, happy girl. All it took were a few sips of a sugary drink, and she sprung up, spinning around, showing off the new flamenco skirt Belen had given her. Although the dress was too big for her, I'd adjusted the waist. She'd insisted on wearing it. And with a red flower in her hair, my daughter looked like a tiny señorita. I stopped at letting her wear lipstick, however, despite her begging me.

I looked at everyone apologetically. "It's the sugar, I think."

Greta and Julien both smiled at my daughter's impromptu dance performance.

"She's lovely. Youthful exuberance is always welcomed around here," Julien said.

He was such a sweet, charming man, and clearly in love with his lovely wife, Greta. They held hands at the table. I felt like I'd stepped into an enchanted mansion where love blossomed in abundance. Everyone seemed so in love, my face hurt from smiling.

When Lachlan and Miranda arrived, we all settled down to a six-course meal. The food was scrumptious. I'd never tasted such tender meat before. And the lobster salad would be something I wouldn't forget in a hurry, with a tangy, creamy sauce that made my skin tingle. Even Ava ate all her vegetables for a change.

I did my best to avoid eye contact with Orlando, who threw me an occasional playful grin. He didn't seem to care. Which shouldn't have come as a surprise, since he'd always displayed that breezy approach to socializing. But of late, I'd seen so many sides to him. Or was that because his true nature was slowly revealing itself?

My inner healer warmed at observing his former easygoing self again. However, as his secret lover, I grit my teeth, terrified everyone would sense the spark between us.

I hadn't brought him a gift, but I had a surprise in store for later.

Orlando was showered with gifts. From books to music, to furniture and paintings. Miranda and Lachlan gave him an artsy chest of drawers designed by Clint in the shape of a female torso, which proved very popular.

Aidan turned to Lachlan. "We haven't seen much of you."

Lachlan put down his knife and fork and took a sip of wine. "I've been working on a development in New Orleans. Not much time to play music. But I'm dying for a session. Maybe later?"

"You can count on it. James brought over the kit earlier."

"Thanks for arranging that. I would've done it," Lachlan said. "I was surfing at the time."

"You're performing later?" I asked.

Aidan nodded. "We thought we'd play some party music."

I nearly laughed. I'd heard their jazz. And while it was brilliant, I couldn't exactly imagine dancing to it.

"Grant should be here soon. He was meant to come to the dinner," continued Aidan.

"They've been to Hawaii. They just got back a couple of hours ago," Clarissa said, before turning to Miranda. "So, are you going to have a proper wedding?"

"Uh-huh. Probably next month. My mother…" Miranda looked at me. "Insists we do it properly."

"Oh, in a church, you mean?" she asked.

"Not so much a church. But some kind of ceremony with my dad giving me away. All the traditional stuff." She smiled.

Lachlan leaned in and kissed her cheek.

"The pictures of their ceremony in Las Vegas are hilarious," I said.

Orlando chuckled. "Sure are. Andy Warhol as the priest."

Clarissa raised her eyebrows. "You're kidding. You hired an impersonator?"

Miranda nodded. "And my god, he sounded just like him. It was crazy."

"Did you film it?" Aidan asked.

Lachlan said, "Yep. Sure did. We'll have you over, and we can all watch it."

"I'd love that," Clarissa said. "I have a thing for the 60s art scene."

"Me, too," Miranda said, looking starry-eyed at her husband. "Lachlan got that oh so right."

I sipped on my wine and, gazing up, I noticed Orlando eyeballing me while he chatted to Lachlan. I was relieved that Clarissa's attention was elsewhere as she welcomed her friend Tabitha, who'd just made a big, noisy entrance.

The Chalmers arrived and a bunch of Orlando's buddies, including a gaggle of giggly girls, some of whom I sensed had slept with Orlando going on how they kept looking at him with teasing smiles. It didn't worry me. I had no right to feel anything about his past. He was a boy. If only my body could remind me of that, because he registered as a man. A hot, virile man. The thought of which made my body burn.

We all moved out to the terrace area by the pool, which opened out to a spacious living area. They had set up a bar with a couple of servers helping the guests to drinks, and the party kicked off from there.

Sherry arrived to take the children back, and after a few protests, they left.

"Your daughter's so pretty," Clarissa said as we lounged back on cushiony seats by the pool.

The night was balmy. A full moon and clear sky had made it ideal for being outside.

"Thanks," I replied.

"She's really talented."

I nodded with my usual upsurge of pride. "She is."

"Her father. I mean…"

"She doesn't know him," I said, largely unaffected.

That question had come up so often, I no longer cared, which wasn't the case whenever Ava asked. That was more awkward. Especially when it involved silly school projects asking kids to construct a picture story of their family.

"Oh. I didn't mean to pry."

"It's okay. I get it all the time." I leaned in and whispered. "A regrettable one-night stand when I was young and stupid." It wasn't the whole truth. But that sounded better than the father being a drug-addicted asshole who broke my heart and my arm.

Her eyes shone with compassion. "I'm sure history's filled with those. I got out of it pretty easily. Aidan was my one and only."

"Oh… wow. That's like Miranda and Lachlan."

"She mentioned that once to me. Mind you, everyone's different. I'm not being judgmental. Take Tabitha…" She moved her head subtly toward her blonde, chatty friend. "She partied." Clarissa raised a brow.

"Somehow that doesn't surprise me," I said, spying Tabitha giggling with one of Orlando's young, buff buddies.

"She's still a hopeless flirt. But she's been with Grant for over twenty years. They're solid."

Just as I looked over at Tabitha, I caught Orlando's eye, and he smiled at me and then his mother.

"Orlando's almost himself again," she said.

"He is."

"Speaking of flirting, has he tried to proposition you?"

Having taken a sip, I coughed. It took me a moment to think straight. I shook my head slowly. I'm sure she noticed my face redden.

"I wouldn't put it past him. He's a player, I'm afraid." She looked at a bunch of pretty girls. "They've all hung out at some point."

"Hanging out" being a euphemism for fucking, I assumed.

"They're all just friends," she continued as though reading my mind. "Except for Chloe." She looked over at a beautiful, long-legged goddess. "She's a model. Ollie pursued her like mad. But I've heard she's saving herself."

"Oh, really? She told you?" I asked. My veins tightened.

Clarissa nodded. "She's part of a group of girls who've decided to go down that old-fashioned path. Allegra has joined up."

"That must break a few boy's hearts. Allegra's a stunning girl."

She nodded. "We've had so many turn up at the house, wanting to see her. Then there's Miles."

"You don't approve?" I'd seen how the pair looked at each other, sharing in the same attraction.

"He's young and so quiet. No one's probably ever going to be good enough."

Aidan joined us. "Who's not good enough?"

Clarissa smiled at me. "We were just talking about all the boys and girls that chase Orlando and Allegra."

He nodded. "It's nice to see Chloe made it."

"We were just talking about Miles and Allegra."

"She could do worse," he said. "He's a good boy. Hardworking. He'll be a scientist one day. Brains are always welcome in this house." He took Clarissa's hand as if making a point. He leaned in and kissed her on the cheek, and she smiled sweetly. Their aura together almost glowed. They were special.

"The age difference doesn't worry you?" I had to ask, unable to resist.

"Five years isn't much. It's what's here that matters." He tapped his head. "If it were up to me, I'd like Allegra to stay with us and be my little girl forever. But that's me being a father." He laughed.

Also living in their own romantic bubble, Lachlan and Miranda almost floated along as they joined us.

"How about if we get some music happening?" Lachlan asked Aidan.

Just at that moment, Sam and his wife Juni arrived to great fanfare. They were a colorful couple, literally. Dressed in a maxi skirt swirling in color and a hot pink ruffled blouse, Juni's bright smile matched her outfit. Holding her hand, her handsome, jovial husband wore a loud graffiti-patterned shirt.

"Ah... the Chalmers," Aidan said.

Orlando joined us and positioned himself by my side to welcome the guests.

Juni kissed Orlando on the cheek. "Hey, birthday boy. I bought you this." She gave him a present. "Hope it fits."

"Let me guess, a T-shirt?" he asked.

"Yep, and a shirt, among other things," she said with a chuckle.

Miles patted Orlando on the shoulder, and suddenly we were surrounded by people.

I stood up. "Excuse me a moment."

I needed a cigarette badly and hated the idea of being seen smoking, so I headed to the garden.

When I moved through the garden, lit up by lanterns, I saw Chloe and her cohort of girlfriends sharing a joint.

"Hey, this is must be smokers' corner," I said, lighting my cigarette.

Chloe offered me the joint, but I shook my head. I was already on edge, and weed made me paranoid. She looked over my shoulder, and I turned and noticed Orlando heading our way.

His pals lifted his chair so that he could join the girls under the tree. When they plonked him down, he looked so relaxed about his situation my heart warmed, despite jealousy clawing its way in.

With her long dark hair and exotic features, Chloe reminded me of Kim Kardashian, minus the curves.

"I see you've met the girls," Orlando said to me.

"Well, only that I just came here to have a cigarette and discovered them here."

He looked at Chloe. "Having a joint without telling me."

I couldn't help but notice how Orlando smiled and joked with her.

I had no right to feel possessive. I was heading for heartbreak if I continued to let myself become too attached.

I needed that job. It paid well. I had a daughter to think of. I just had to toughen. If anything, as his nurse, I needed to encourage Orlando to enjoy himself.

But as a woman, my emotions played another game. Scattered and confused, they kicked all sensible reasoning in the head. Especially when I saw Chloe's elegant, slender fingers with those long red nails land on his arm and remain there.

"I guess I better get back to the party," I said.

Orlando was sucking on a joint and laughing at something when I left.

I felt so old and ugly as I lumbered off. I couldn't help comparing my short and dumpy self to the tall, svelte model.

10

ORLANDO

It was interesting seeing Chloe again. Although she was as stunning as ever, with that long raven hair and big dark eyes, I'd lost interest. Considering how I'd chased her, that struck me as odd. But everything about me had changed. I was no longer that boy who'd go hard for something he couldn't have.

Perhaps on a deeper level, I thought she'd never be interested in me now that I couldn't walk.

Strangely enough, however, she seemed more attentive. She was all smiles and touches, stroking my arm more than once.

Maybe it was pity? That girl had cock-teased me to the point of madness. We'd kissed. But, being devoutly religious, she wanted to wait until she married. At the time, I'd wanted to fuck her pretty badly. But not that badly.

She hung by my side as we headed back to the terrace.

My mother joined us. "Are you having a nice time?" She turned to Chloe. "Lovely to see you. How have you been?"

"Good. I did a screen test for a Netflix show the other day, and it went really well. I've got a good chance, apparently."

"Oh... I didn't realize you were breaking into acting," my mom said.

"I took some lessons in New York while on a modeling job."

My attention drifted to Harriet. She chatted with an older guest, who, going by how close he stood and that eager gleam in his eyes, was coming on strong. Why wouldn't he? She looked hot in those figure-hugging jeans.

Chloe's silky hair touched my shoulder as she bent down to whisper, "I'll be back in a minute."

I went over to Harriet and spoke to our neighbor. "Hey, Doug, do you mind if I have a word with Harry?"

"Harry?" he asked.

"That's me," Harriet chimed in. "Short for Harriet."

"Oh... of course." He looked at me.

I cocked my head. "Come on. Let's have a cigarette away from the crowd."

Harriet looked at me like I'd shown her something a complex math equation.

I shook my head. "What?"

"What happened to your leggy model?"

"Are you jealous?" I grinned.

She bit into a nail. "I'm your nurse. I have no right to be."

"You've got a right to be human." I gazed into her eyes.

She continued to make a meal of her nail and remained quiet.

I knew well enough how sex complicated relationships between buddies. But with one's nurse? The potential repercussions were too dirty to contemplate. Like the fact that my family paid her to care for me. And that giving blowjobs had become a valuable component of her duties. Those pretty lips giving the best head I'd ever had, and I'd had my fair share, outweighed any immoral implications.

Harriet gripped the handle of my chair. Light-headed after the joint, I didn't mind her pushing me along.

We headed to the quiet part of the house, away from the guests. "This will do," I said.

She lit our cigarettes. "I hope your parents don't see us."

"No one comes here." I wrapped my arms around her firm, curvy thighs. "Sit on my lap."

Harriet wiggled out of my hands. "No. Not here. I need this job. And someone might see us."

I kept grabbing at her legs, and eventually she fell onto my lap. Our mouths collided and then I tripped off on her soft, beautiful lips. My fingers crept under her blouse, sliding over the curve of her breasts, while our tongues danced together.

A bush rustled, and Harriet jumped off my chair like she'd touched a live wire.

I laughed. I didn't really care. I couldn't have been the first to fuck my nurse.

Harriet adjusted her top. "We should go back. Everyone will be looking for you."

"You'll come back to mine later. Won't you?"

She nodded. "I've still got a present to give you."

When we returned to the party, some guests kept at me to perform my latest material. Even though I felt the songs weren't developed enough, I agreed. My father grabbed a guitar for me, while Miles accompanied on the piano and Lachlan improvised on a set of bongos lying about.

Performing made me high. Better than any drug I'd ever tried. Even though the audience were mainly family and friends. The thrill of improvising live appealed to my inner adrenaline junkie.

After performing four songs, we ended the short set to rapturous applause. I couldn't stop smiling, knowing the songs had been well-received.

Miranda came up to me and said, "Hey, that was awesome. I'll have to book this act for one of our functions at the Artefactory."

Harriet joined her and nodded. "You'll have to come up with a name."

"How about 'I want to fuck my nurse?'" I whispered.

Her face went red. "Shh… not here."

It was after midnight when I headed over to Harriet's cottage and called out in a loud whisper. It took a few goes before she finally came to the door.

"It's okay, you don't have to whisper. Ava's staying at the castle," she said, stepping down from the porch.

"The castle?"

She laughed. "That's what she calls Miranda's home."

"Oh… I suppose it is. Like our house."

"Oh, yeah. This place is like a castle, all right."

I stared up at her. "Why don't you come over? We can have a coffee to wake up."

"Okay," she said with a flicker of a smile. "I haven't given you your present yet."

"I don't care about that. Just get your sexy ass over here."

She placed her finger in front of her lips. "Mary," she whispered, tilting her head toward the cottage next door.

"She's cool. She's heard it all before. This used to be my bachelor pad once."

Harriet grinned. "I can imagine."

I smiled at her dry tone. Those wild days were behind me. Even if I could, something told me it would be different from now on. Seeing Chloe had made me realize I was no longer that boy anymore. Legs or no legs.

"I'll be there in a minute," she said.

I headed back to the cottage and put on some music.

It had become easier to do things, like raising myself up from my chair. That action in itself seemed like a miracle.

Harriet tapped on the door.

"No need to knock," I called out.

She came through, and I had to do a double take. "At last, my nurse has arrived." I grinned.

Harriet's tiny nurse's uniform barely covered her ass, and I was on fire.

I tapped my knee. "Come and sit here."

"Don't you need your temperature taken," she said, bending over.

I was about to question that, since she didn't normally take my temperature, but I soon realized it was part of the act. "Sure. You better. You'll find it's a bit on the high side."

She placed her hand on my brow, and I laughed. "The wonders of modern science." I went to pull down her front zipper, and she slapped my wrist.

"Mm... naughty," she said.

"This little uniform is sexy. Do they really wear these? Because the hospitals would be full of horny patients."

"It's a 60s uniform," said Harriet, adjusting her dress after it had ridden up. "I got the smallest one I could find. It's a bit tight."

"Mm… it is. Very nice." I pointed to the floor. "I dropped something over there."

Harriet grinned and bent over, exposing her naked ass.

"You forgot to wear your panties. Naughty nurse," I said.

"I had an emergency to attend to," she said.

"Let me think. A desperately horny patient?"

She sat on my lap and laughed. "Uh-huh."

I lowered the zip, and her breasts fell into my hands. "Oh, god. No bra. Can we keep the uniform as part of this job description?"

Harriet moaned as I teased her nipples with my tongue. "What about the regular visits from your folks?"

"Mm… that could be an issue." I nuzzled into her breasts. "Why don't you take me to bed, Nurse Naughty."

"Nurse Naughty?" she laughed and rose, pulling her uniform over her ass.

I virtually came on the spot. Talk about hot.

Once we were in my room. I pointed at the bed. "Sit there and spread your legs."

Harriet had gone heavy-lidded. She was just as aroused as me. Her pink, juicy slit made me salivate.

"Nursie is horny. She's seen her patient's hard dick," I said.

"I haven't, though, have I?" She smiled sweetly.

I unzipped my fly, and my cock sprung out. "There."

She ran her tongue over her lips and then placed her fingers on her clit.

"Wider," I said.

I played with my dick, watching as she fingered herself. My erection burned, pre-cum lubricating my sliding hand.

She ran her tongue over her mouth once too often. "Down on your knees. Now." I pointed to the floor.

Sinking to the ground, Harriet took my cock in deeply. Her tits hung halfway out of her uniform, making it hard to think.

My head dropped back from intense pleasure, while her fleshy lips moved up and down, sucking and licking my cock like it was delicious candy.

I stopped her. "I want to taste you and then I want to come inside of you." I placed my weight onto my arms and got myself onto the bed with little effort. "Why don't you sit on my face."

She frowned. "Really? Won't I smother you?"

"No way. Do it."

"You're getting bossy," she said, squatting on my face, while holding the headboard. I licked her bud, and she shivered, but I held her there and lapped my tongue slowly over her swollen clit.

She groaned. "Stop. It's too much."

I continued to ravage her until I tipped her over the edge. She trembled and came on my tongue.

Harriet fell by my side on her back, her mouth parted and gasping. "Holy shit. That was insane."

"Turn over," I said, dying to ride her from behind, which had become possible since gaining strength in my thighs.

"Yes, sir." She giggled.

I entered her with one deep thrust and her pussy sucked my dick in and devoured it. My heart pounded in tandem with my penetration, working up to a speed that promised to rip my head off.

I drove my cock in hard against her firm, curvy ass.

Seeing her in that uniform, with her tits hanging out, had made me crazy desperate.

An orgasm shot out of me like a cannon-ball. It was so insanely mind-blowing, I cried out. I'd never done that before.

There was no doubt: Harriet had well and truly raised the bar. I fell onto my back and panted. "Holy fuck."

I turned on my side to look at her beautiful, rosy face.

"Hey. You were using your legs. Did you notice that?"

"I was too focused on getting my senses off the ceiling to notice." I laughed.

"You're getting stronger all the time." She rose from the bed. "Stand up for a minute."

"Huh?"

"Just do it," she said. Our power had shifted; she was the bossy one now. But I was so high that I didn't mind. I liked it. I liked her.

I made my way to the edge of the bed.

Harriet took my hand. "I've got you. Just stand up."

Although my legs shook, I didn't need her support for once.

I widened my eyes. "I can do it."

Harriet covered her mouth. "Oh, my god."

I took a few steps before my legs gave way, and I sat down again. But I'd turned a corner for sure.

"Your muscles are weak," she said. "But in the coming weeks, they won't be. Starting tomorrow, we're going to work out harder. Weights and all."

"It did feel easier. And I didn't need you to hold me up. Did I?"

She shook her head and bit her lip. "You're going to walk. I'm absolutely positive."

"You're not just saying that?" I asked, even though a part of me felt it, too.

"Nope. I studied it. Paraplegics can't do what you've just done. It was inflammation for sure."

"Great birthday present," I said.

Harriet remained pitched at the side of the bed.

"Let's sleep," I said.

"I can't stay here. Your parents might pop in early," she said. "Or they might knock on my door."

"Just crash here with me. I want you to. Get up early, if you like. It's been a big night, no one will be up and about until later."

Harriet joined me in my arms, and I fell into the most contented sleep I'd had since the accident.

11

HARRIET

A week after the party, like a miracle, it happened: Orlando walked. He had crutches for support, but I knew it was just a matter of time before he'd manage without them.

Clutching her husband's hand, Clarissa cried while Aidan bit his lip.

"I couldn't have done it without Harry," Orlando told them.

They regarded me with a glow in their eyes. Although Clarissa showed something more than just appreciation. Her slightly furrowed brow made me wonder if I'd worn my top inside out.

I headed over to Miranda's house to pick up Ava, where I found her playing in the garden with Manuel.

A cold sensation swept through me in the realization we'd have to return to our dowdy apartment. What a huge comedown, after being lavished with billionaire comforts. Although I'd psyched myself up for this moment, I still couldn't fight the blues at the thought of leaving.

With that fairylike garden and beach as her playground, what about Ava?

How could I do better than that?

"Mommy, look what I made," she said, taking me by the hand and leading me to a goddess statue draped in a floral chain.

"That's beautiful. You're so clever." I kissed and hugged her. "Come, let's go and see Aunty Andie."

I found Miranda on the terrace staring down at her laptop.

"Hey, there," I said.

"Harry, I heard," she said.

I nodded. "Lachlan dropped in just as Orlando was moving around on his crutches."

"It's amazing. So, he'll make a full recovery?" she asked.

"He sure will." I smiled, recalling the moment. "It was amazing when it happened."

"Tell me about it."

I took a breath. "Well, it actually happened after we got together on the night of his birthday. And since then, we've spent every day working out hard at the gym. He's getting stronger all the time."

"Oh my god, that is so great." She studied me for a minute. "So, how do you feel?"

"I'm totally stoked, of course." I paused to take a breath and still the swell of emotion forming in my throat. "I'm a little sad this is about to end, though. Lucky, I kept the condo."

"Hey. You can come here and crash on weekends with Ava. Lachlan loves having her here."

"That's sweet. But wouldn't we be in the way?"

"Hello. Have you seen how big this house is? And there's Sherry. She takes the kids out and helps." She smiled coyly. "And, I'm going to need more help soon."

"Why?" I asked.

Her smile grew.

"Oh, shit... you're not are you?"

She nodded. "Uh-huh. Two months, I think."

I hugged her. "That's so great. Have you told Mom and Dad?"

"Last night. We went over for dinner."

"How's Mom with Lachlan?"

"You know. Lots of questions. He likes her. He thinks she's bright and amusing."

"Amusing?" I asked, scrunching my forehead.

She giggled. "Lachlan likes difficult people."

"Mom's not exactly difficult... She's just critical."

"That's what I meant."

"When's the wedding?" I asked as that little bubble of excitement was pricked by jealousy.

I hated myself for that. But didn't misery like company? After that high of Orlando walking again, I'd crashed.

Would he keep seeing me now that I was no longer his nurse?

"We talked about having a ceremony here. In a month's time. Before I become too fat for the wedding pics."

"That sounds good. So how did our parent react to that idea?"

"Mom didn't say much. She was still getting her head around me being pregnant, I think. As you can imagine." Miranda chuckled. "But Dad was ecstatic. He and Lachlan hit it off straight away. It turns out that Lachlan loves the *National Geographic* channel. And he's also a huge David Attenborough fan, just like Dad."

"Christmas should be fun." My dry tone made her laugh.

After I grabbed Ava's overnight bag, we said our goodbyes, and Ava skipped by my side.

"Sweetie, we're moving back to our old apartment," I said.

She stopped walking and looked up at me with her lovely big blue eyes, which always seemed filled with wonder. "Oh? But we can still visit Aunty Andie and Manuel. They said I could stay whenever I liked."

"Of course. And we will."

She shrugged. "Oh well. I don't mind. It's closer to the studio. And to school."

"It is, darling." I stooped down and hugged her. "I love you, sweetie. You're such a good girl."

She smiled like an angel, and my spirit thawed. My daughter's happiness was all that mattered.

When we arrived, I spied Orlando on his porch, chatting with Chloe, and my heart sank.

We'd fucked every night. Each time, it was a game. I'd go to leave, and he'd clutch my hand, all heavy-lidded and horny. And within a breath, I'd a slow strip for him.

He made me sink onto his big dick and ride him, my eyes watering from the sheer pleasure of him filling me to that point of bursting. How could any man compare to Orlando?

It wasn't just the sex, however. He fitted me like a warm comfy coat on a cold day. I loved being around him. We'd spent every day of the past three months in each other's company. Even when he got into one of his crappy moods, I still wanted to be there.

And now, I was staring at a long-legged beauty laughing with him and looking like a part of his furniture.

"Hey," he said. "You remember Chloe from the party?"

I nodded. "Hey." I shifted from one leg to another. "Okay then, have a good night."

My emotions were in a tangle. It was the first night I hadn't hung out with Orlando. And what was I to do? He didn't really need me anymore.

Instead of packing, as I should have been, I sat at the table staring into space when Clarissa came to my door.

"Hey. Sorry to disturb. But wondered if you had a moment?"

"Sure, come on in." I stood away from the door.

Clarissa smiled at Ava, who was having a conversation with her doll on the couch. She returned her attention to me. "It might not be a great time for a chat. Um... can we maybe speak tomorrow?"

I looked at Ava and said, "Go and play in your room, sweetie." I looked at Clarissa. "Now's fine."

I needed to know what she had to say. I couldn't wait another day. It was time for us to move. It needed to a quick clean cut.

"Can I offer you anything?" I asked.

Clarissa shook her head. She touched my hand and her eyebrows drew together. "You've been great. I am sure Orlando wouldn't be walking so soon had you not pushed him."

"Thanks. And look, I get that he's going to be okay from this point on. He'll be without those crutches any day now."

"I think so, too." She nodded. "We're eternally grateful."

"We'll pack up and be out of here in a day."

"Take a week if you need. We'll miss not seeing Ava. She's a gorgeous girl. You should be proud."

The lump I'd gulped back earlier had returned. I had to do some deep breathing to speak. "No. We're good. I think by tomorrow. I've got a few jobs I'd like to apply for," I lied.

I had no plan, and the thought of returning to the hospital where my journey with Orlando began, filled me with dread.

Having risen, Clarissa hovered. I sensed there was more she wanted to say. She knitted her fingers. "Sure. We'll make sure you're paid an extra four weeks."

"That's so generous of you. I mean..."

"No. Please. You've been great. You've pushed him over that line." She took a deep breath.

"What is it, Clarissa? I'm sensing something here."

"Look, um… I had some photos sent to me. I'm not sure from whom. But someone from the party, I can only suppose."

"Oh?" I asked. My heart pumped so hard I felt dizzy and fell back into my chair.

"They're photos of you on Orlando's lap, kissing. I deleted them. Aidan doesn't know."

I released a trapped breath. That made me feel a tiny bit better. "Right. Look. We'd been drinking. I'm sorry. It just happened."

"Don't worry. I understand," she said softly, touching my hand. "I'm not surprised. I've seen how Orlando looks at you. Aidan noticed it, too. I'm only telling you this because I don't want you to get hurt. You've done so much for us."

I smiled tightly. "I'm not attached. He's young… and well, we'd been drinking." I opened my hands. "I'll leave tomorrow. All will be forgotten." I harnessed the strength of Thor to fight back tears.

"Orlando's always worried me. The way he flirts and breaks girls' hearts. He takes after his grandfather. I can't stop him from being that way. That's what having money can do to people, I suppose. Anyway, I noticed Chloe is over there now. I hope you're going to be okay."

"You're so kind to worry about me. I'm totally fine. I'll miss this gorgeous place, as will Ava. But there's Miranda next door. I'm sure we'll see you guys around."

We hugged, and I saw her out.

I'd packed and had everything ready for the move in the morning. I loaded the car so we could head off early. I was keen to get going. In a way, I was looking forward to getting back to my roots.

I was a downtown girl. I liked being in the city. Losing myself in crowds. And there were a ton of gorgeous guys I hadn't met yet. I took a deep breath and, although my heart ached, I was ready to take on the next chapter of my life.

Ava came running out, and I hugged her. "In the morning, we go back home. Are you good with that, sweetie?"

"Yeah. I suppose. I will miss Miranda's castle, though."

"We'll visit often."

"And when we're back home, we'll go to the park where all your friends play."

She smiled and did a spin into the splits. Feeding off her joyful innocence, I found myself smiling for the first time that day.

When a knock came to the door, I found Orlando leaning against a walking stick.

"Hey," I said, opening the door. "This is a surprise."

He stepped through the door. "It sure is. It feels so weird to be moving again. Great, though."

"How are your legs? Are they sore?"

He touched his hips. "Around here."

"Your hip flexors. That's why you must stretch your quads and hamstrings religiously," I said. "It's great that you're now only needing a walking stick. This morning you were on crutches."

"I needed those for balance. But I'm getting better all the time. I might go down for a swim tomorrow."

"Don't rush into it," I said, touching his hand.

His eyes softened as he touched my hand. "I hope we can catch up still. I'd like to see you again."

I nodded slowly. "Sure. Maybe. I mean, I'm kind of looking for more than casual. And you're young… and there's Chloe…"

"She's someone I once liked. I'm not sure now. I'm not sure about anything. This accident has changed me. I know that I'm hot for you, though. Last night was really off the charts. Every night has been. Especially my birthday. That will be unforgettable."

A smile trembled on my lips. His eyes had that bedroom shine, I recognized well enough. But this time, I wouldn't surrender.

"Someone sent a photo to your mom of us smooching."

His brow creased. "Shit. Really? I wonder who."

"Probably Chloe. She was rather cool toward me, and she had this look in her eyes, as though she knew about us. Even earlier, she was a little standoffish."

"Chloe?" He shrugged. "I don't know. I mean, she dropped in to see how I was. Which is weird."

"Why?" I asked. "She likes you. That's plain to see."

"Mm…" He grabbed my hand. "I'm going to miss you. I mean, I'm not going to miss not being able to walk."

He looked older than twenty-one. What he'd endured would age anyone. I just had to keep reminding myself that he was young, and we were on different paths.

I turned away to fight back tears. "I best keep packing. I'll be leaving early in the morning."

He grabbed my hand and stopped me from moving away. "Why don't you come over? It's your last night here. We can listen to music and have a few laughs and you can…" He tilted his head with a cheeky smile. It was easy for him. Life now offered endless possibilities. Whereas my life was back to heavy lifting and hard work.

Oh, how I wanted to jump on his lap and have his mouth all over mine. But I had to stay strong. "I can't. Ava's here. I promised we'd watch a film together and grab a burger."

"What are you watching?" he asked.

"I don't know. *Cinderella*. Something cute like that. Must have a happy ending and no mention of sex or guns."

"Sounds good."

I looked at him, and his grin made me laugh. "You'd hate it."

"Not if you're here. Come on. I could do with some greasy burgers. All those healthy meals are making me feel dull." He rubbed his stomach, and his T-shirt flicked up and showed me the tanned six-pack my fingers loved sliding over.

Ava came out with her Barbie doll. "She's got a new dress. Mommy made it for me."

"Wow. That really suits her," he said, looking impressed. He turned to me. "That's clever. I didn't know you sewed."

"You don't know a lot about me, I guess," I said. "We need to go for the burgers. It's close to tea time for Ava."

"Sure." He stood up slowly, and I noticed he had a slight tremor but adjusted himself by holding onto the chair.

"Are you sure you're not too unsteady? I'd hate for you to fall," I said.

"Nuh… I'm good. Real good." He clapped his hands together. His joviality stung like sun on light-deprived eyes.

"Can I join you?" He raised an eyebrow, denoting more than just burgers and film-watching.

What could I say? I recalled Clarissa. "I kind of promised your mom…"

"We're grown-ups." He touched my hand, and sparks tingled up my arm. "I'll drop over in an hour."

Falling into his dark playful eyes, I took a deep breath. "Sure." I smiled tightly. I couldn't resist. I wanted him badly. One more time. And we *were a*dults.

We returned with burgers and fries, and I turned on some of Ava's favorite cartoons.

As I studied my beautiful daughter, a sense of purpose came over me. I was a mother first. And my daughter was going to do great things. I knew that. I would put all my energy and focus on her. Not as an ambitious showbiz-mom but as a nurturing, supportive one.

We giggled at the road-runner and the coyote, when a knock came to the door. Ava jumped up and ran over to open the door.

Orlando wandered in carrying a six-pack. "Has the movie started yet?"

We watched Cinderella up to when Ava fell asleep. I carried her to bed and tucked her in.

I returned and stood by the TV. "Do you need to keep watching?"

He shook his head and tapped the couch. "Come and sit next to me."

I'd had a couple of beers and felt tipsy as I sat next to him. He took my hand and played with my fingers.

We fell into each other's eyes and, like the pull of a magnet, I fell into his chest. He wrapped his arms around me and held me.

"I'm going to miss not having you around. We've been seeing each other every day for months," he said.

"As your nurse," I corrected.

"Yeah… as my sexy nursie." His eyebrows lifted. "That little uniform will become a feature of my wet dreams."

"I feel bad about this. I promised your mom."

"Hey. Let's not go there again. You're moving tomorrow, and if we want to hang out today, we will."

I let him crush me with warmth and his lips touched mine for a fragile kiss. That's how it felt. For me, at least. There was guilt, confusion, lust, and yearning all rolled into one.

It had to be our last time. Orlando had a bright future. A musical career. A filthy rich family who could give him everything. And the ton of women that came from him not only being wealthy and talented but also hot.

His tongue entered me deeply. The heat of his arousal set my heart on fire, as an overwhelming ache to be ravaged shivered through me.

He slid his fingers under my blouse and caressed my breasts. "You've got the sexiest tits." He rubbed himself against me. I felt his hard dick, and I was a goner.

"We better do this in the bedroom," I said.

Our lovemaking was hard, driven, passionate, and hungry. And when it was all over, we nestled into each other's arms.

"I'll have to visit you," he said.

"You want to keep seeing me?"

He pulled away from my arms and regarded me. He always looked older after sex. Or was that me justifying us?

"Why not? We've got a connection. I mean, I can't promise anything."

"But there's Chloe and girls and…"

"So?" he asked.

I studied him. He looked almost blank, as though we were talking about going for a walk.

"You mean like fuck buddies?" I asked.

"I suppose. I'm not a fan of that term. I like you more than that. But I'm not ready. And now that the legs are back…"

"Back to partying?" I asked.

"Not as wild as once, but it will be good to get out."

I unraveled from his arms.

"Where are you going?" he asked.

"I don't think it's a good idea you crash here, Ollie."

He rose and rubbed his head. "Sure. You don't want Ava to see me. I respect that."

"Not just that. But I feel bad about breaking my promise to your mother."

He turned to look at me. With that tousled dark hair and sultry dark eyes, Orlando had the kind of looks that broke hearts.

Mine.

"I love my folks. And Mom means well. As you know. But it's none of her business."

We hugged, and I walked him to the door. "This was probably a bad idea." I paused to find my words. "I've developed feelings." I stared down at my feet.

He kissed my cheek. "I like you, too." He trapped my eyes, and intensity swallowed the air between us. "Let's take each day as it comes."

Wise words, I thought. And filled with hope. Even if my heart hadn't quite caught up, especially after seeing him all chummy with Chloe. I kept telling myself he deserved a girl like her.

I watched him hobble off. It warmed me knowing that he was going to be okay. That's all that mattered. A boy as talented and vital as Orlando deserved that.

It was seven when we left the following morning, without saying anything. I left a 'thank-you' card and flowers I'd picked up the day before for Mary and Clarissa.

I didn't even say goodbye to Orlando, who I assumed was still sleeping.

Ava acted so bravely. It was also hard for her. How could it not affect her? She wasn't made of stone, which was how I felt. Every step came with effort.

The simplest task like picking up milk along the way back to our ordinary lives nearly made me cry. I was that drug addict who'd had their last taste, and now my emotions convulsed from relentless cravings.

After I dropped Ava off, I headed to my favorite café and sat there, watching people bouncing around, giggling, and basically enjoying their lives.

I ordered a muffin and coffee and held my cheek while observing life strutting along with purpose. It was a bright sunny day and as noisy as any Monday morning.

One thing I knew for certain: I needed to reinvent myself. I'd given so much to Orlando's recovery, my tank was empty. I needed a break from nursing.

12

ORLANDO

Lachlan ran out of the water with his board under his arm. "Hey. Good to see you standing there."

"Good to be standing here." I sat on my towel.

"Are you going in?" he asked.

"I'm not ready to surf yet. But I've had a few swims. When it's not too rough."

I couldn't bring myself to admit that I'd become a pussy. Something back in my wild, conquer-the-world days, I would never have imagined possible.

Even if it took a shrink, I would jump on that board again.

"That looked great out there. That last wave was awesome," I said.

"Yep. Sure was." He dried his face and drank some water. "So, is everything back to normal?" He pointed at my legs.

"Pretty much. I mean, I can't run or walk for long distances. But I'm training all the time. I'm just fucking relieved. Every day I thank someone."

"God, you mean?" he asked.

I shrugged. "I've gotten deeper. I'm searching for something, I suppose."

He nodded slowly. "I know what you mean. I've got Miranda and music and this." He pointed at the ocean. "That's all the spiritual nourishment I need."

I smiled. Love, music, and the sea made sense. But would that be enough?

"How's married life treating you?" I asked.

"Great. I'm really happy. We're happy. Miranda's pregnant."

"Oh, wow, man. Congrats. You're happy about that, I imagine."

"Sure am. I'm over the moon. We're just arranging the ceremony. That's if I can survive my mother-in-law."

"She's bossy?" I asked.

"You could say that." He chuckled. "She's smart and doesn't take crap. In many ways, I like that kind of woman."

"Me, too." I poured sand through my fingers.

"Are you playing at the Red House tomorrow night?" he asked.

"You bet. I can't wait."

He picked up his board. "I've got to get back. Miranda's organizing a show at her gallery, and I promised to help. Since Ethan left for New York, she's in need of a bit of muscle." He flexed his biceps. "By the way, there's an opening on Saturday night, if you're interested."

"Will Harry be there?" I asked.

He nodded. "She's working there in admin. Miranda's employed her."

"Really? She's not nursing?" I asked.

"Nope. Harry said she needed a break."

"I probably wore her out." I dropped my grin. "I suppose you know we hooked up?"

He nodded. "I've known from the beginning."

I took a deep breath. It had been two weeks since I'd seen Harriet, and I missed her. I'd never missed a girl before. And missing Harriet didn't go with my plans to pursue a musical career.

"Has she said anything?" I asked.

"Miranda hasn't." He studied me. "Are you falling for her?"

I shrugged. "Maybe. I don't know. It's not a good time for me. I'm not ready for a relationship. And there's Chloe."

"Are you still chasing her?"

"Not really."

"I suppose you've got six months to catch up on where girls are concerned."

"I didn't really do without for that long," I said with a guilty grin.

"Ah... Your nurse."

"Yep. And you know what's really strange, I'm not in the mood to fuck around. Weird, yeah?"

"Then maybe you have fallen for Harry. You could do worse. She's a great girl. A bit crazy at times. And loud."

I smiled. "That's why I like her. She's down to earth."

"Come to the exhibition on Saturday and catch up. I'm sure she'll be happy to see you."

I nodded. I suddenly realized there was a family function, which included Chloe. "Shit, there's a dinner. I promised. Mom invited Chloe, too. I think she's trying to get us together. She wasn't too pleased about me being with Harry."

"She found out?"

"Someone sent her pics of Harry on my lap," I said.

"Who?"

"I don't fucking know." I scratched my whiskered jawline. "It's time I moved."

"The estate's huge."

"It is. But we're too close-knit as a family. I love being here. But I need privacy."

He nodded. "That makes sense. You wanna go wild."

"I was doing that before. But I kind of like Harry. I wouldn't mind dating her for a while. In that no-strings attached way."

Lachlan stared at me for a moment.

"What?" I asked.

"She's looking for a relationship, I think."

I shrugged, leaving it at that because I couldn't work out what I wanted. One step at a time, since I'd only just started walking again.

"I'll see you at the gig tomorrow." I waved and headed back, trying to come up with an excuse for skipping Saturday's dinner. I couldn't even recall what it was for.

I was starving and headed back to the kitchen where I found my mother.

"Hey, Mom."

"Darling." She wore a bright smile. "How was the beach?"

"Good. I didn't go in. It was a bit rough."

She returned a sad smile.

"I went in yesterday. I'll surf again."

"If you don't ever again, I won't be too upset."

I smiled. "I know." I grabbed a banana. "Is lunch ready? I'm starved." The smell of baking in the air made my stomach do somersaults.

"Any minute now. It's just us and…"

"And?"

"I've invited Chloe."

I studied her for a minute. "I know what you're doing."

She headed into the dining room and arranged the plates.

"Where's Mary?" I asked.

"She's having a day off."

I sat down at the table. My legs ached. "Speak to me."

She looked at me. "Chloe's a nice girl. And I remembered how much you liked her. It could be healthy to have a steady girl for a while. You've partied pretty hard up to…"

"Up to my accident," I said, finishing her sentence. "I know. And I wouldn't mind partying a bit more. I'm only now allowed to drink."

"I'm not suggesting you settle down or anything."

"But that's what a steady girlfriend is. Settling down."

She shrugged.

"This is about Harry, isn't it?"

"I like Harriet. She's a good person. But she's older, and she probably wants a relationship with someone. That's only natural."

"We're not like that." It was better to keep my hookups to myself. My stomach still knotted. "I'd had a bit to drink, and it just happened that I pushed her onto my lap. That's all. There's nothing more to it."

My mother took a deep breath and held my stare for a moment. "Darling, I saw you leaving her cottage the other morning. I know you've been together. And look, it's all good. You're an adult. Chloe told me she'd developed feelings for you and, remembering how much you liked her, I thought it would be nice to have her here."

I exhaled. "I need a life away from here. I know you mean well. But I'm not ready to marry Chloe. Or have a relationship with anyone for that matter."

"Darling, I know you're not ready to marry, but I thought it would be nice to hang out with someone you liked." She paused. "You've changed. You've become more serious and focused. It's a good change. You're maturing."

I nodded slowly. "I have changed. Do you think Dad would mind if I moved into his apartment in Venice?"

"I can't see why not. You'll have to ask him." She stared at me. "Promise me you'll continue with your music."

I followed her back into the kitchen where a steak and vegetable pie set off a delicious savory aroma. I almost floated in the air like a cartoon character toward it.

"I'll never give that up. I wanna record an album."

She hugged me. "Darling, I want what's best for you. So does your father."

"I know that. I'll come back and forth. I love it here. It's our little paradise."

Her eyes misted over. I could see that talk of my moving affected her.

We sat down to eat when Chloe arrived. She was a beautiful girl, but I was no longer a boy who chased what he couldn't have.

"Hey," she said.

I leaned in and kissed her on the cheek. "Hey."

"You're looking well." She smiled brightly and handed chocolates to my mother. "They're homemade."

"That's nice of you. Thanks." She took the box.

After lunch, I invited Chloe for a stroll in the grounds.

"You seem to be moving well," she said.

"I'm getting stronger every day." I stopped walking and faced her. "Did you send that photo of me and Harriet to my parents?"

Her dark eyes widened. "No way." She tilted her head. "Are you having sex with your nurse?"

"She's no longer my nurse."

"From what I gather, older women have a certain allure."

"She's not that much older. Only five years."

She studied me. "You still like her?"

"I do. We've been through a lot together. And she helped me walk again. I'll never forget what she's done for me."

"Oh… so do you feel you owe her?" she asked.

"No fucking way." I had the sudden urge to be alone, so I could pack and move into the penthouse that same day.

Chloe grabbed my hand. "I'd like you to be my first." She bit her lip. "I've always liked you. You were just too much of a player."

I scanned her tanned face and traveled down her body. Although she was supermodel thin, she was very beautiful. Any hot-blooded male would have fallen over himself to bed her.

"It's a big responsibility, Chloe."

She laughed. "I don't want you to marry me. I just want you to be my first."

As I continued to study her, I felt nothing. It wasn't Chloe's pout that she kept running her tongue over, or her long legs in that tiny denim skirt turning me on. My dick slept until Harriet's short nurse's uniform came to mind, making it stir.

I leaned in and pecked her pillowy lips before stepping away. "It's not happening for me, Chloe."

"Oh…" Her smooth brow wrinkled. "You're not able to since the accident?"

If only she knew how I'd fucked my nurse every which way possible. The thought of which fired me up. I wasn't going to fuck a virgin and take the responsibility that came with that, while fantasizing over my former nurse.

"This just isn't the right time. Now or here." I was just craving a session with my guitar.

She moved away. "Sure. Sorry for coming on a bit too strong."

"It's all good." I smiled. "I'm flattered. You're a gorgeous girl. Boys were, and I'm sure still are, crazy about you."

She touched my hand. "I'd still like it to be you. I'm not expecting a serious relationship. Perhaps we can catch up again."

I nodded. "Why not?"

13

HARRIET

The Artefactory had become the place to be. After seeing so many patrons turning up with paper cups, I thought it wise to sell coffee. In his typical can-do fashion, Clint embraced the idea with enthusiasm and, within a few weeks, we'd set up a café and also obtained a liquor license.

Sam Chalmers supplied his very popular craft beer, and the gallery boasted a steady flow of colorful characters and hipsters.

I once viewed the art scene as pretentious, but I enjoyed my new role. At least, there were no patients screaming at me and sleep-deprived, grumpy doctors giving me hell.

There was so much to do and learn I didn't have time to dwell on myself—that pathetic girl, pining endlessly for a boy. Even though physically, Orlando was very much a man. And mentally, too. He possessed a sharper mind than most men I'd hung out with. But then, I'd met five-year-olds brighter than some guys I'd dated.

Jackson Chase came through the door, lugging a painting.

Swaggering toward me, Jackson was forty going on twenty-one. Mm… funny about that. Who said age was a construct?

"Hey, beautiful," he sang.

"Jackson." I nodded, keeping it professional.

Now that Miranda was pregnant, she'd passed the gallery running to over me while she sourced new artists and negotiated the financial terms for exhibitions.

"Can I squeeze this into the collection?" he asked.

I stared up at the crowded walls. "I don't know where you're going to fit it."

"I'll find a way."

I shrugged. "Sure. Knock yourself out. The opening's tomorrow night."

He rubbed his hands. "Can't wait. I have a good feeling about this. This place rocks. I've come to all the shows. It's always a good night."

I had to agree. The exhibitions were more of a party than a commercial venture, despite the sell-out shows.

I was proud of Miranda. Even my mother had become a convert. She loved dropping in and chatting to whoever was there. Rolling her eyes at our modern speak, as she liked to call it.

"So, Ms. Flowers. Dinner?" Jackson asked.

I looked down at my watch. "It's only eleven in the morning." I smirked.

"No. I mean, Saturday night. We can celebrate after I sell out tomorrow night."

"You're pretty confident, aren't you?"

"What? About asking you out? Or selling out?" His eyes lit up playfully.

"Both." I headed to the office to see about the catering.

"You're single. I'm nearly single. Why not?" he added, walking by my side.

"'Nearly single' is why." I cocked my head. "I've got to keep moving. Got lots to do. Clint's out the back somewhere. He'll help you rearrange your paintings."

"Okay. But I'll keep asking." He raised his eyebrows.

Jackson was hot. But I was off men. I needed to focus on my career and being a good mother.

After I'd arranged everything for the Saturday show, I headed off to pick up keys for a condo I'd rented close to the gallery. The seventies condo was so spacious, I was in heaven. The pink walls in Ava's room-to-be sold me. Airy and bright, and freshly painted, I loved the living room. As I fell onto the sofa, anticipation soared through me. There was nothing like a fresh start to pump the promise of possibilities through one's veins.

Things were looking up for me. And instead of crying myself to sleep, I now sprung up out of bed with a purpose.

My phone buzzed and seeing it was Orlando, I picked up.

"Hey," I said.

"What are you up to?" he asked.

"I'm sitting on my new couch admiring the blue walls in my new place."

"Is it good?"

"It's great. And it's close to the gallery and walking distance to Ava's dance classes."

"Sounds handy," he said. "What are you up to later? Do you feel like catching up?"

How I wanted that booty call, which is what it always was between us. "I haven't got time. I need to move in by the weekend. And I have an exhibition opening tomorrow night."

"Do you need a hand moving?" he asked.

"I'll let you know. How are your legs?"

"I'm almost there. Had a swim today, which felt good. And even the waves didn't freak me out as much."

"I'm glad. Beach bums need their surf."

He laughed. "This beach bum's recording an album."

"I can't wait to hear it."

"We'll have a launch. And you'll get an invite."

"I have to run. Too much to do," I said. "Are you coming tomorrow to the exhibition?"

"I'll try. There's a dinner. It's Chloe's birthday. I promised I'd go."

Blood drained from my face at the mention of her name. I had to suck it up, reminding myself I had no right to be jealous.

He'd spoken to me, face-to-face, about us being friends with benefits. All I could do was fidget and look away as he gently explained with a slight stammer about going out with Chloe and her friends. The last thing I wanted him to feel was guilt.

Despite remaining deadpan, my way of hiding behind a smokescreen of pretense, I felt my heart freeze. Holding my hand, he'd explained how he loved being with me, but at the same time he wasn't ready for something serious. I just shrugged it off as though we were talking about the weather.

One smoldering look from those large dark eyes and I opened my thighs willingly. The inner strength I'd once possessed had fled. Instead, I closed my heart down, telling myself it was just fucking. Feverish, heart-pounding sex.

Before Orlando, I'd never had an orgasm while penetrated. In the same way I was addicted to nicotine, I craved Orlando's dick.

But we also philosophized. His book-loving grandfather had instilled in Orlando a mercurial outlook on life. At times, his words seemed anachronistic, like he'd stepped out from the past.

But then he'd return to being a boy. His eyes sparkling with life, especially since being able to walk again. I loved how his face lit up when he spoke passionately about music, and how he'd explode into superlatives when describing his favorite guitarists. Yelling things like "Holy shit, that's insane" over some guitar solo while we lounged back listening to records.

As a remedy to this heart-versus-body tussle, I'd convinced myself, like I did about cigarettes and junk food, that I'd give him up soon.

"Are you there?" he asked.

"I am. I better run. Bye."

I took a deep breath and headed back to my old condo to continue packing.

My parents arrived early and took a tour of the new exhibition. "It's colorful," my mom remarked.

I smiled. That would have been my comment once. But since being around art, I'd learned more about the subtleties of modern art and had developed a taste for it. Not all paintings appealed. But as Miranda kept reminding me, if the crowds liked it then our views were best kept for our personal collections.

The large canvases were a series of colored splotches against stark backgrounds and even gifted, I wouldn't have hung it on my walls. But Jackson Chase's work was popular, and that's all that mattered.

I hugged my dad and kissed my mom. "You're the first here."

"We're unfashionably early." My dad chuckled.

Clint joined us and greeted my parents. "The bar's restocked and the champagne's ready to pop, and everything's set."

"Lovely."

Miranda walked in with Ava at her heels.

"Thanks for picking her up," I said.

"No problem." She gazed at the walls. "They're a bit crammed."

"That's Jackson for you. He turned up yesterday with a new painting, and he had to include it."

Ava ran over to me. "Hello, sweetie. How were dance classes?"

"Fun. I'm learning a grown-up's dance."

Miranda nodded. "I watched. She was amazing. Lachlan's still there. He's helping his mother."

Our parents joined us, and we huddled together.

"I'm proud of you girls. This is such a marvelous place," my father said, taking a glass of champagne from the waiter.

Miranda looked at me and smiled. "The Flower sisters are rocking."

I laughed. It felt nice.

Orlando was still in my life. Not in a committed way. But he called every day without fail. I just had to stop obsessing about Chloe, and any other pretty girl that swanned into his life.

Jackson arrived, followed by a crowd, as the caterers dropped off the canapés.

Miranda, my mother, and I arranged them on a table, and within thirty minutes, the place was buzzing.

Clint's brother and sister took over the bar, and we helped with clearing plates and glasses.

Although the gallery was making good money, I liked to get in there and get my hands dirty, as did Miranda. And my mother just couldn't stay away. It gave her something to do, other than teaching. Like me, I think she enjoyed the novelty of something new, and likewise, she just loved the place.

By seven o'clock, all the paintings had sold, and cash register symbols rung in my eyes. I wanted to see the gallery thrive.

It was around nine when my parents took Ava. She was to staying with them over the weekend while I moved everything into our new home.

Jackson approached me, clutching a bottle of champagne. "Can I top you up?"

I held out my glass. "Why not? It's been an outstanding success."

"Hasn't it?" He looked around. People chatted, laughed, and raved about his abstracts.

"So. About that dinner." He touched my hand just as Orlando walked in with a couple of friends, one of which was Chloe, giggling and rubbing shoulders with him.

I returned my attention to Jackson. "What's the score with your wife?"

He opened his hands. "We're separated."

"But you're still living together, aren't you?"

"For now." He held my gaze to test my reaction. "This show will mean I can now afford my own apartment."

Despite my heart fluttering for the gorgeous younger man coming toward me, I accepted it was time I grew up and hung out with men my age or older.

"Ok. It's a date," I said.

He leaned in and kissed my cheek. "I look forward to it. Next week, then?"

"Sure." I peered over his shoulder. Miranda beckoned me while Lachlan chatted with Orlando.

"Excuse me." I left him and went to join Miranda.

Noticing her plate filled with snacks, I said, "Wow. You're hungry."

"I'm eating for two. And I can't stop. Look at me, I'm exploding."

I laughed. "You're not even showing, crazy girl."

"Yeah, but I'm still stacking it on."

"Your tits are bigger," I said.

"Tell me about it. Lachlan can't keep his hands off me."

"Mm… I bet. You two are like rabbits in heat." I chuckled.

"Jackson's married, you know," she said, munching away.

I removed a cheesy snack from her plate and placed it in my mouth. Unlike Miranda, I'd gone off food, which I put down to angst. I bit into it, and my stomach contracted as a warning. I returned it to her plate.

"Hey," she protested.

"I have no appetite."

"Orlando?" she asked.

I nodded with a sigh. "This fuckbuddy arrangement is no longer working for me."

"Chloe's pretty determined," she said.

"Have they fucked?" My nausea intensified. "She's a virgin, apparently. She's keeping herself for the right man."

"Oh, really?" Miranda snuck a peek. "She's pretty."

"Rub it in, why don't you."

"Look, Harry, he's a boy."

I nodded. "In age, maybe. But he fucks like a man." I got hot just thinking of our recent hookup.

When Orlando arrived after midnight last night, I had to let him in. My hormones had the upper hand. The scorching need in his eyes as he fucked me deep and hard still blinded me.

"What's the story with Jackson?" she asked.

"He kept asking me out, so I accepted. Anyway, he's now separated."

"He's a player, you realize? That's why his marriage broke down. He's a cheater."

"Who's a cheater?" Orlando asked, joining us.

"The guy that's got the hots for Harry," Miranda replied.

I rolled my eyes.

I liked that Orlando knew I had other options, even if I'd promised myself never to play games. But I couldn't help it. I ached for him to react. After all, jealousy was love's psycho sister.

Love? And there it was, that endless, enough-to-invoke-a-premature midlife-crisis question: Was I in love with Orlando?

I had two options, either join a Buddhist retreat or revert to my former Tinder days.

Orlando leaned in and kissed me. "You look hot."

His scent shot through me like a drug. I nearly turned into a puddle, seeing him looking all buff, with those strong arms. Only a few nights back, I'd bitten into them as he fucked me senseless.

Adding to his animal allure, Orlando had grown a short beard. He used to border on beautiful. Now, he was brain-meltingly hot. And I liked the way his whiskers prickled my skin whenever he trailed his tongue along my inner thigh.

"You brought your girlfriend along, I see." I slid my gaze over to Chloe, whispering to her buddy.

"That's her girlfriend."

"She's pretty. They're all are," I replied with a snarky sting. So much for remaining cool.

"They're not as sexy as you, Harry," he said with those dark come-to-bed eyes. "Anyway, they're girlfriends as in more than just friends."

"Oh." That brought a smile to my heart. "Is Chloe gay?"
"Nope. She's bi."
"And her girlfriend doesn't mind you being there?"
He shrugged.

I rubbed my lips tightly in an attempt to stem the emotional torrent flooding my brain. "So does that mean you're fucking both of them?"

His eyebrows knitted. "We're not meant to be doing this."
"Doing what?" I shifted my weight.
"Talking about who's fucking who."
"So, you're fucking Chloe, then?"
He nodded and shook his head at the same time.

I jerked my head back. That was it. Fuck the cool act. We'd been through enough to share everything, including whose DNA Orlando had swallowed that week. "Well, which is it?"

"We've tried."
"Tried?" I squeezed my brow.
"It just didn't work for me," he said.

It was like enticing a fasting sugar junkie with a decadent chocolate dessert. My curiosity was not just aroused but teased to the point of madness.

Straightening my spine, I managed to suck it up and joined Jackson instead. "Excuse me."

Orlando grabbed my hand. His eyes held me hostage again. "Hey, you're not pissed at me, are you?"

His unflinching stare penetrated so deeply that tears burned at the back of my eyes. I looked away quickly. "I have no right to be angry. This is a bad idea."

"What is?" he asked.
"Us."

Before he could respond, I headed over to Jackson to arrange a get-over-Orlando fuck. I needed out. And the only way out would be in the arms of another man.

14

ORLANDO

We put the finishing touches to the last song on our new album. It had been a month of daily studio sessions and it had paid off. We were close to releasing an album. There was a slight jazz feel, but I'd stuck to R&B with a hint of folk for a couple of ballads.

The studio team used the term "commercial gold." They seemed pretty buzzed out by what we'd produced.

Miles was the king of riffs, whereas I found my jam writing lyrics, melody, and segues. According to the producer, my singing voice recorded well. Apart from guitar and piano, we used drums and bass guitar—a standard four-piece band.

The music was organic; we went for the raw, no bells and whistles approach because I'd insisted on keeping the production down to a minimum. No digital overlays. Just four musicians recording in an old-fashioned way. If it was good enough for The Rolling Stones and The Beatles, it was good enough for us. At least that's what I told Zane, the guy at the desk who was in his early seventies and had worked with some of my favorite 70s artists.

Sitting behind a panel of glass, Zane said, "I think we should lower the bass on the intro."

Having repeatedly listened, I'd lost the ability to be objective, so I left it up to him. I'd hired the best in LA and respected his judgment.

By day's end, I was exhausted and headed back to my place.

I'd moved into my father's penthouse in Venice. I liked being there. It gave me a chance to spread my wings now I'd become an adult who could walk.

I still visited Malibu regularly. That was where my soul lived. At least, my parents still had Allegra, which came as a relief. Otherwise, my mother would have smothered me. She already did enough of that.

My father, the cooler one of the pair, understood that I needed to find myself through the world of music, women, and life.

I'd visited Harriet twice that week, but she'd refused to see me after telling me she was seeing Jackson.

That pissed me off. He had player written all over him. Which seemed hypercritical, since she wouldn't see me because I'd asked for us to remain casual. Although my body was hooked, I needed to do a ton of things before having a steady girlfriend.

Chloe buzzed, and I let her in.

I preferred to keep things on friendship terms only with Chloe. Even though Harriet had closed the door on us, I felt a little numb where other women were involved. Maybe I wasn't allowing myself to admit how I really felt about my former nurse. But the next stage meant all in. And I had too much to do with my life before I could commit to anyone.

After Harry had pushed me away, I'd agreed to catch up with Chloe. We'd had a bit to drink and the next thing she attempted to suck me off. Her teeth got in the way, and not in that blood-pumping, gentle scraping fashion as Harriet had mastered. Chloe kept pulling a face, as though she hated having a cock in her mouth. I couldn't blame her. I wouldn't want one in my mouth either. But I'd been spoiled rotten. Harriet ate my cock like it was a fucking banquet. And boy did I crave her sexy mouth.

I told myself to stop comparing them.

With Chloe, I got the feeling she just wanted to hook up with someone rich. I'd told her I couldn't commit. But she kept calling anyway.

Chloe looked around the room. "Hey, I love this place." She stepped onto the balcony. "The view's awesome."

Wearing denim shorts and a tiny tank top, she looked even skinnier. The way her ribs jutted out concerned me. I hoped she wasn't starving herself.

We stood there for a moment as I often did, watching the parade of weirdos and beautiful people. It was a game of "spot the normal person" along the boardwalk.

"Can I offer you a drink or something?" I asked.

"Just some water, thanks." She followed me back in.

"How's Melanie?" I asked after her girlfriend, handing her a glass.

"She's in New York doing a Dolce and Gabbana show." Chloe studied me as though trying to piece together some mystery. "Are you still stuck on Harriet?"

"I like her. And we've got good chemistry. She gets me." I paced about. After six months of sitting, I preferred to feel my legs, especially with the recurring nightmares of me in a wheelchair hurtling down a steep drop.

"So why are you seeing me then?" she asked.

"We're just hanging out, aren't we? And anyhow, Harry's called off our arrangement."

Chloe's dark eyes penetrated mine. "You're no longer fucking?"

I shook my head. For some reason that grated on me. It was more than fucking. Harriet was someone I could be myself with. She hadn't judged me, even after at all the shit I threw at her.

"You seem unhappy about that," she said.

"I like her."

She joined me and stood close. "Do you like me?"

"I do. I've known you for ages."

"You were chasing me for years. Now you can have me."

"Look Chloe, I don't know. The other night..."

"You're really big," she said.

I shrugged. "I haven't had too many complaints." I thought about Harriet. The fit was perfect. She had a very wet, responsive pussy. I got hard just thinking about that heavy-lidded look in her eyes and the way her lips parted when I entered her.

I loved talking dirty, but all this talk about dick sizes was putting me off sex. Insane really for a self-confessed sex junkie that I'd always prided myself in being. But that was me as a boy. I was now a man whose legs were getting stronger by the day, and who had a thing for his ex-nurse.

"Why do you want me to be your first?" I asked.

She shrugged. "I want to try it with a guy. I feel like I can trust you."

"But aren't you into your girlfriend?" I asked.

Chloe looped her hair on her finger. "We like each other."

"And she doesn't mind?"

Her mouth trembled. I sat down next to her and took her hand. "What's wrong?"

"She's seeing a guy too. Melanie's into polyamory."

"I see." I stared her in the face. "You should tell her how you really feel."

A tear fell on her cheek. "She knows. And then there's my parents."

I rose, grabbed some tissues, and handed her a couple. "They're pretty religious, aren't they?"

She nodded while blowing her nose. "That's why I thought with you…" She sighed heavily.

"Hey, it's fine. I get it. You wanted to try it out with a guy and at the same time make out you've got a boyfriend."

Chloe frowned. "It sucks, doesn't it?"

I went to the fridge and grabbed two bottles of beer. "Can I offer you one?"

"Yes, please."

I joined her again, twisted the top off, and handed her the bottle.

"Thanks." She looked up at me with teary eyes. "I'm sorry for involving you. But you also didn't seem into it, either."

I shrugged. She got that right. My dick seemed half asleep.

"Harriet?" she asked.

"Yep," I puffed. "It's not meant to be this way. I've got too much to on. But I also don't feel like being with other girls."

"Is that why you don't find me attractive anymore?" she asked.

"You're gorgeous, Chloe. That's all you have to know. It's a two-way thing, hooking up. And let's face it, you weren't that keen either."

We remained silent for a moment.

"It's okay to be gay, Chloe. This ain't the fifties."

She rubbed her lips together, lost in thought. "I know. It's my parents. I'm the only child. There's so much expectation and pressure. A grandchild. A trophy husband."

I laughed. "I'm hardly that."

"You're the catch of the century, Ollie. You're fucking rich, and good-looking."

"Hello. Party boy central. Remember all those sex videos and shit about me. Unless they were living in a cave, they must have heard."

"They're very fifties in their attitude. It's cool for a guy to be wild but not for the girl."

"Double standard, ah?"

"Welcome to the real world, Ollie. Just because we've caught up, doesn't mean our parents have."

"I guess you're right. My dad's really open, but my mom wants to see me with a nice girlfriend. That's why she keeps inviting you over for lunches and dinners." I chuckled.

"If only she knew which side my bread was buttered."

"I won't say anything unless you do."

She smiled. "Hey about the other night. I'm sorry for coming on really strong. I could see you were in a dark place."

"It's okay. I should've stopped you. But I thought maybe I could be my old self again. But he's gone. I hardly know this new me." I drained my beer.

"You broke a few girls' hearts back then, so it's probably a good thing that you've dropped the bad-boy act."

I sniffed.

Her mouth curled for the first time. "I can't understand the blowjob allure, though. No offence."

I laughed. "Neither can I. I'd hate to suck a dick."

We looked at each other and laughed.

I could only conclude that all those teenage years spent pining for Chloe had been nothing but the delusional yearnings of an overactive ego driven by her constant rejections.

After I saw Chloe out, I headed for the balcony with my guitar and plucked away as I watched life prancing along.

I'd decided to have a break from girls. Music would be my one and only lover for now. We had an album to launch, and I was dying to play jazz gigs again. My soul craved music more than anything else.

15

HARRIET

"Mommy." Ava skipped along as I strolled through the gardens of Miranda's mansion. "Will we move into our own castle soon?"

I smiled sadly. "Not quite yet. But I'm sure when you grow up, you'll move into a castle."

Was I being a bad mother for filling my impressionable daughter with unrealistic expectations?

My mother was on my back to ditch the princesses and knights in shining armor, and teach Ava about the real world. But as my angel leaped about, picking flowers and chasing butterflies, my heart kindled at the wonder and magic of innocence. I couldn't see any harm in dreaming of castles, swishing ballgowns, and crystal slippers. I enjoyed it, since I relived my childhood vicariously through my daughter. It put a smile on my face. Without her, I would have been a crumbling mess.

"Don't you like our new place?" I asked.

"I do. But I like it better here," she said, looking up at me with her big sparkling eyes.

"We'll always visit Auntie Andie. And you'll get to stay here as often as you like."

She whirled. "Yay."

We found Manuel in the garden kicking a ball around.

As Ava ran over to play with him, I yelled, "Don't dirty your nice, new dress, sweetie!"

"I won't," she said, chasing the ball Manuel kicked toward her.

I shook my head. That new pink dress did not stand a chance. At least, I had a change of clothes, since we were staying the weekend.

It was my first time back since moving from the Thornhills. I did everything to push Orlando away from my thoughts. And there was Jackson. We hadn't caught up yet, but he'd become my moving-on-from-Orlando remedy. Shame my heart didn't skip a beat around him.

I stepped onto the terrace and met Sherry.

"Hey," I said. "Where's everyone?"

"Miranda's upstairs getting ready, and Lachie's surfing."

"On his wedding day?" I asked, laughing.

"That's Lachie for you." She chuckled.

"Is there anything I can do to help?" I asked.

"No. The caterers are here now. They've got staff to do everything. We're just meant to have fun."

"I've never seen you with a drink, Sherry," I said.

"Oh, I have my moments," she said, tipping her head.

I looked down at my watch. "When are the guests due?"

"In two hours."

"Okay then, I'll go and see what Miranda's up to."

I ran upstairs and knocked on her bedroom door.

"Come in," she called out.

The enormous room resembled a gallery, just like the rest of the palatial home. Miranda couldn't stop buying art. Abstracts, landscapes, and nudes crowded the yellow walls.

My sister stepped out of the bathroom, wiping her lips. "I'm so fucking sick."

In sympathy, my stomach contracted. "I'm not too well myself. Must be something I ate."

"Really?" She frowned.

My period hadn't arrived either. Changing the subject, I regarded the silky gown on the bed. "Is that what you're wearing?"

"Yep. What do you think?" She lifted it up.

"It's lovely. It suits you."

Wearing shorts and a loose T-shirt, she sat for a moment. "I'll have to take some anti-nausea tablets just to get through it."

I smiled. "You'll forget all about it once everyone's here. And this is your day, sis. You're getting married."

"We're already married. It's more of a party. A celebration. I mean Lachlan's surfing. He's so relaxed about everything. Unlike me."

I flicked through albums covers by the turntable. "Who's entertaining?"

"We've got a jazz outfit." She smiled. "Surprise, surprise. But there's also a DJ. And with so many musicians around, I'm sure they'll perform. It will be fun."

"How many are coming?" I asked.

"There's around a hundred or so I think. All the neighbors, friends of Lachlan, and I invited all our cousins and relatives."

"Shit, all of them?" I asked. My mother had five sisters. All devout Christians.

"Have they been warned?" I asked.

She undid her braid and brushed her hair. "Yep. They know there'll be alcohol."

"Why did you invite them?" I asked. The last time the sisters got together, it was hell. All their lecturing on the evils of alcohol made my poor father, who was a moderate drinker, have to sneak his beer and bourbon outside.

"Mom suggested it. I think she wants to rub their noses in it. They're all so snobby. And with Mom being the least successful, they've always made a point of putting her down for not marrying a lawyer."

"They hate me. I'm a sinner in their eyes for being a single mom."

"Let's just ignore them and have fun," she said, running to the bathroom.

Her retching became contagious, and I joined her.

That's how Lachlan found us both, with our heads down the toilet.

"What the fuck?" he said, standing there with wet hair and wearing nothing but his shorts.

I rose from the ground and left Miranda on her knees. "I must have eaten something bad."

I read concern in his eyes as he looked over at Miranda.

"Can I get you an iced tea? I know I need one," I said.

Lachlan wrapped his arm around her.

"That would be nice," she said. "I'll see you down there. I've got something I can take. Do you want an anti-nausea pill?"

"I better. I need to eat. I didn't eat much yesterday, either."

Lachlan and Miranda looked at each other.

My chest knotted as dizzying fear drained blood from my veins. "I'm not… I don't think I am." I looked at Lachlan. "Don't say anything to Orlando about this. Please."

He opened his hands. "Hey. It's none of my business."

I left them and headed downstairs.

Two hours later, the guests started arriving. Our parents were the first through the door.

My mother moved around the house as though she lived there while our dad and Lachlan chatted. They had a good connection. Miranda had told me that Lachlan viewed our father as the father he wished he'd had. Apart from their fascination for nature shows, they also loved watching ball games.

All in all, it was a great marriage, and I was so happy for Miranda, who looked like a princess in her crimson floaty gown with a lace bodice and a flattering tulip-shaped line.

Ava was over the moon as she danced about. Her dance teacher Belen had arrived with her younger guitarist boyfriend. They'd been together for five years now, I was told. And she was thirteen years older. For some reason, that made me feel better about me and Orlando. Despite him not being ready for a girlfriend.

I wasn't looking for a husband, but I didn't want to share him either.

I'd bought a fifties-inspired dress with a fitted bodice and full skirt. A white rose sat by the side of my pink-streaked hair. Ava, who'd made a habit of wearing flowers in her hair, suggested it. Clarissa and Allegra, with their elegant and unique dress styles, had rubbed off on me.

Orlando strode in, and my face flushed. Judging by the way he moved with ease, I could tell he'd made a full recovery. My heart sang to see him restored to his former self.

He cut such a deliciously handsome figure in a tux, and he turned every woman's head. He looked much older. With his dark hair styled off his face, Orlando would have made a perfect James Bond. Especially with those chocolate grinning eyes and swarthy features.

Even my puritanical cousins, who weren't as innocent as their mothers' thought, ogled.

Orlando leaned in and kissed me on the cheek. "You look stunning. You haven't been answering my calls."

His intoxicating herbal-infused cologne stole my tongue, and the ground seemed to sway beneath me.

"I've been busy moving into a new place, and the gallery's keeping me on my toes."

He stared into my eyes. I sensed he wanted to tell me something, but people surrounded us.

Clarissa and Aidan were close. I wasn't too concerned about Aidan, but Clarissa, as much as I liked her, made me uneasy.

His eyes smoldered into mine. I'm sure others noticed. Friends didn't normally look at each other that way. The delicious burn between my legs brought it all back as his inappropriate and undressing gaze lingered.

"It's a great dress. You look amazing," he said, touching my hand.

It was such an intimate gesture that I flinched, removing my it quickly.

"You look handsome in that tux," I said. "And you seem to be moving freely."

"I'm back to my old self."

While he continued to transfix me, longer than socially appropriate, I gripped my legs to stop them from shaking.

"Excuse me," I said.

The wedding was about to start, and I badly needed the bathroom for some breathing space to still my racing heart.

Ava came running over to me. She had a big stain on her dress. And I shook my head. I shouldn't have let her dress so soon.

"What's that?" I asked, lifting a chiffon layer.

"We had some chocolate ice cream," she said, biting her lip.

"Mm... come with me. Let's see if we clean it up."

"But it will make it wet," she lamented.

"We'll use the hair dryer."

I took her little hand, and we headed for the bathroom. One of the many joys of having a child, my daughter helped me forget about all my issues.

And boy, did I need a distraction. Orlando's eye-fucking had gotten me all hot and bothered. Had it been somewhere dark and away from everyone, I would have seduced the pants off him.

I cleaned Ava's dress and, with the help of a hair dryer, we saved the day. After I brushed her golden waist-length mane, I pinned white and red flowers in her hair.

Handing her a basket with a floral arrangement my mom had made, I stepped away to look. "You look lovely, sweetie," I said, kissing her. My eyes misted over. She was such an angel.

Manuel was showing Dad his toy truck when we returned to the guests. The small, handsome boy wore a tailored suit, while his proud grandmother Belen watched on.

As Ava stood next to him, everyone gushed over how cute the pair looked.

"We have a surprise later," Belen said, removing a loose strand from Manuel's brow.

My mother, who'd been chatting with Clarissa's dad, Julian, turned and studied Ava, and noticing the flowers in her basket had come unstuck, she knelt down and rearranged them.

She then turned to me. "Where's that photographer?"

"He's taking photos of Lachlan and Miranda." Just as I said that, Miranda came in and said, "I want photos with all of us."

The photo shoot was fun. Orlando kept pulling silly faces to make me laugh, which was captured on photo. He really was a child. But then I enjoyed it, as did Ava, who was making all kinds of ridiculous poses.

"Ava, stand normally," I said.

"No," Lachlan said. "Let her pose. That's more fun." He looked at his gorgeous mother, who looked striking in a red dress with a flouncy hem. "You, too, Mom. Pose all you like."

She shook her head with a slight frown. "I'll save the dance poses for posters."

What an interesting collection of people we made. It was hard not to smile for the camera.

Under an arch of twining roses, Miranda floated along a red carpet with her arm looped in Dad's.

Her lips trembled. She glanced over at me, painting a "is this real?" grimace.

The celebrant read a poem that Lachlan had written, which was actually very moving and well-crafted. When he attributed those heartfelt words to the groom, everyone looked at Lachlan.

He cocked his head. "I can do other things than just surf."

Everyone laughed.

Even my mother was impressed by his words, giving a subtle nod of approval.

After the ceremony, the party really kicked off. My hunger had returned, and I filled my plate and sat down on one of the many tables arranged in the garden. Being a perfect summer afternoon, the grounds made for an ideal setting.

Orlando stood by my table. "Do you mind if I join you?"

Wearing a grin, he seemed so at ease, which was the opposite of me.

Nerves aside, I gestured for him to sit.

"You haven't eaten for a while?" he asked, pointing at the mound of food on my plate.

"No. I didn't eat much yesterday. I'm making up for it today."

"You've lost a little weight," he said.

"That's always a good thing." I stared down at my plate to avoid his searing gaze.

"You don't need to lose weight. Your body's perfect."

I plastered a smile. "Thanks. Yours isn't too bad either."

Our eyes held, and it wasn't just the delicious banquet I wanted to devour.

Allegra swanned over in a purple silk gown, which I assumed she'd designed. In the flourishing garden, she could have been part of a *Vogue* spread.

"Nice to see you again, Harriet," she said.

I stared at the golden-haired beauty and smiled. Miles stood close by her. As another older woman, younger man connection, they seemed so natural together, and happy.

When she moved away, I said, "I see Miles is still hanging close to Allegra."

"They're together now," Orlando said, matter-of-factly.

"Oh, really? He's five years younger."

He spread his palms. "So? Anyway, it's not official between Miles and Allegra. But I know."

"They're young."

"I think they'll last. Allegra's always been loyal and traditional in many ways. So's Miles. They're very similar."

"Are you loyal and traditional?" I asked.

"I'm too restless to be traditional."

"I've always known you were restless."

He leaned in close. "Hey, I didn't fuck anyone else while we were together. And not since, either."

I nearly choked. "I was always there, Ollie. It was easy."

"It meant more to me than that." He looked down and fidgeted. "I still think about you."

Just as he gazed up at me, Clarissa and Aidan joined us. I nearly spilled my drink. I was so drawn to Orlando, I hadn't noticed their approach.

Aidan asked, "How have you been, Harriet?"

I took a deep breath and prayed they hadn't noticed my jumpiness. "I've been great." I smiled brightly. "The gallery's going really well."

"That's a great setup. I enjoyed the last show. Well done," he said.

"Miranda deserves that more than me. She's made it what it's become. I'm just working alongside her now that she's expecting."

"Does that mean you've given up nursing?" he asked.

"I think so. For a while, anyway. I needed a break."

I regarded Clarissa, and she smiled sweetly.

Lachlan arrived and spoke to Aidan. "How about a session? The instruments are all set up."

"What about the bridal dance?" I asked.

"My mom's got something planned later, I believe," Lachlan said.

"You're going to dance flamenco?" Aidan asked. His surprised tone made me and Clarissa giggle.

"No. But, she's arranged a performance with the children."

"Ava's been practicing like mad," I said, shaking my head. "The neighbors aren't too happy to have us there."

"How is your new place?" Clarissa asked, looking sympathetic.

"It's okay. A step-up from my other place. And it's close to work."

She smiled and left me to join her chatty pal Tabitha, who was sharing a giggle with Juni Chalmer.

I went in search of Miranda and found her with Allegra.

"Hey, that was a moving ceremony," I said.

Allegra nodded. "Wasn't it? And those lovely vows."

"They were. Even Mom was impressed," Miranda said with a chuckle.

"When's the bridal dance?" I asked.

"We'll have some fun later. They're about to play now," Miranda glanced over my shoulder.

"What about the bouquet toss?" I asked.

She touched her mouth. "Oh, I forgot. Thanks for reminding me."

I watched her heading to Lachlan who was adjusting the peddle to his drum kit.

She returned and made an announcement, and the younger crowd huddled together giggling and making a fuss.

My mother touched my arm. "Aren't you going to join them?"

"Nah. I feel stupid."

Refusing to accept my pathetic excuse, she pushed me into the fray and I found myself positioned next to Allegra, who I smiled at me with a shrug.

Miranda signaled Lachlan, and he played a drumroll. She turned her back to a bunch of giggly guests and tossed the flowers high in the air.

At first all I could see were the girls, and Clint, who wore the most outrageous orange and purple suit I'd ever seen, scrambling about screaming.

As it was, the bouquet barreled straight toward me. But instead of catching it, which I could have done easily, I stepped out of the way and the flowers fell into Allegra's hands. She cast me a frown, and I shrugged it off.

Everyone applauded and seeing Miles close, I noticed stars in his eyes as he watched on. Clarissa hugged her daughter and whispered something.

I turned and noticed the band had set up with Orlando, head down, tuning his guitar.

There were three generations of Thornhills: Orlando, his father, and grandfather, Grant. All the while, Lachlan sat at his kit saying silly things and making them laugh.

"Are you going to play?" I asked Miles as he stood by Allegra.

He looked at Allegra and then nodded. "You bet."

"I gather you're dating?" I asked her.

She nodded shyly. "We are."

"How long?"

"Um… about a month now."

"And your parents are okay?" I asked.

"We haven't exactly announced it. But I'm sure they've guessed. They like Miles. I think they were hoping I'd go for someone my age, but I'm only five years older. And to be honest, it doesn't feel like that."

I knew exactly what she meant. "Age is so personal. I've met forty-year-olds who act like they're fifteen and twenty-one-year-olds who act forty."

Allegra nodded, wearing a sympathetic smile. I sensed she knew about me and Orlando.

"Hey, by the way, that bouquet was headed straight for you," she said.

"Doesn't matter." I patted her arm. "You're more deserving."

"Everyone deserves a happy marriage. But hey, thanks."

I returned a smile. I didn't want to catch the flowers to avoid the fuss. That was all there was to it. Or at least, I told myself that.

The music started, and we all headed into the main room where servers had set up a bar. Despite the relaxed feel of that reception, no expense had been spared in the food and drinks, and the place buzzed with a party atmosphere.

Being early evening, the pool shimmered under the darkening turquoise sky, where silhouetted birds glided, and the salty air offered a warm kiss. It felt great to be alive, regardless of life's little challenges, like falling hard for one's younger patient.

R&B music headed straight to my hips and proved so contagious that many of the guests danced, including my mother who'd broken into a jive with my dad. I loved seeing her letting her hair down. And she had a lot to smile about. Miranda had married a friendly billionaire, a grandchild was on the way, and an in-laws open-house arrangement.

Clarissa, Juni, and Tabitha shimmied and swayed their gorgeous bodies as we all laughed and had a ball.

Every now and then, I stole a glimpse of Orlando, dripping in charismatic rock star with his white shirt half-hanging out of his fitted black slacks and his top buttons undone. With his eyes closed, he performed a seductive solo. His pelvis grinding against his guitar.

Acting more like teenagers, Miranda and I danced with our arms up high. Ava swirled and leaped about while Manuel busted some pretty cool moves and melted our hearts with his big-eyed grin.

After that, we sat down to a five-course meal, and Lachlan gave a moving speech. He described the night Miranda accompanied him to a ball in a shit-brown dress that she'd been forced to wear, and stole his heart, making us laugh and cry as he opened up about his feelings for my sister.

After we drank to their health, a floor show began.

Ava had told me all about it, so I knew what to expect, but it still dazzled.

Lachlan's mother performed a flamenco dance with her boyfriend accompanying her. Her rhythmical footwork synchronized perfectly with his fiery strums. The performance ended in a wild climax and she swirled into a statuesque pose. Her arms stretched high and chin lifted to the guests' "Ole!"

Ava and Manuel followed with a duet that had everyone shaking their heads in wonder. My face hurt from smiling. They were little stars.

After Orlando joined Javier, the guitarist, to play more flamenco, Belen dragged Miranda and Lachlan onto the dance floor, among my sister's protests.

He played the part by raising his arms and banging his feet. His mother had obviously shown Lachlan some moves, and it was so entertaining to watch, especially with that silly grin on his handsome face.

Lachlan wrapped his arm around Miranda's waist and spun her around. They ended facing each other, moving their hips and arms.

The guests clapped along, and it became so raucously wild and hilarious that Miranda just danced along as best as she could. I loved the impromptu nature of that supposed bridal waltz.

Aidan and Grant joined on guitars and drove the gypsy music in a frenzy of rhythm that was so intoxicating I found myself swirling and stomping on the dance floor with Ava.

It ended up being such a great party that come midnight, the guests left with big smiles.

Orlando met me outside for a cigarette, which I stubbed out after only one puff. It tasted awful, which struck me as odd. I'd been trying to break that habit for a while.

"I didn't realize you played Spanish guitar," I said.

"Neither did I?" He laughed. "I just improvised. But it's exciting to do. And you were exciting to watch. You're quite the dancer."

I laughed. "It's called champagne."

"It's been a great night, hasn't it?" he said. "It's still warm. Do you feel like walking down to the beach?"

"I'm crashing here tonight, and I'm not that tired." I looked at him in the moonlight and his eyes wore that melting softness that made my heart gulp.

I knew what us being alone on that beach under the moon would lead to. And I went willingly because I was a woman after all.

"Isn't this amazing," he said, pointing to the shimmering silvery beam as we walked along the path.

"It sure is," I said, sitting on the sand. "I was expecting Chloe as your date."

"Why?" He sat next to me. "We're not together."

I studied him closely. I'd learned to read his face after all those months together as patient and nurse. He often kept his responses vague or would give me the silent treatment. Although I didn't miss his grumpy, angry outbursts, I did miss him needing me. Selfish as that was.

"Oh, it's over between you?" I asked.

He sifted sand through his fingers. "It never started."

I turned to face him. "You haven't slept together?"

He shook his head.

"She's hoping to rope you into marriage first?"

"Nope."

I was dying to know more, but his curt responses stopped me.

He stroked my face. "And what about you? Are you seeing Jackson?"

"You know about him?"

"I was at the gallery. I met him." His mouth turned up at one end as though he'd tasted something bad.

"You didn't like him?"

"Nope. He's a douche."

"Why would you think that?" I asked.

"Because he's got an ego the size of LA, and he's still married and playing you at the same time."

"They're separated. I'm not really that interested. I just need someone to take my mind of you."

His fingers skimmed over my arm, making my skin prickle.

"I'm not interested in Chloe. It was a game once. She's not like you."

As his hand slid over my arm and close to my breast, my body heated, and my nipples hardened in anticipation.

He brushed his lips with his tongue. They had sex written all over them and, before my next breath, our mouths touched. That kiss was soft and warm and so inviting I levitated to a blissful state where nothing mattered but that moment.

His tongue entered deeply, and his tender kiss became savage.

He groaned in my mouth as he felt my breasts. Unzipping my dress, he unclasped my bra, and they fell onto his palms.

"I love how you feel, Harry. I've missed you." His deep rasp penetrated to my core as he rubbed his crotch against me.

I unzipped his pants and took his hard, throbbing cock into my hand.

"I can't stay away from you," he said, sucking my nipples.

Before I could speak, he opened my legs roughly, ripped off my panties and trailed kisses up my thighs.

His tongue landed on my slit, swirling and lapping my clit like it was a banquet and making me flinch from oversensitivity. I dropped my head and shuddered a sigh.

The intensity of his licking turned me into a whimpering mess. My pelvis rose to his lips and a hot toe-squeezing release blinded me with fire.

I tried to move away before I lost my mind. But he brushed and nibbled at me until all the warm ripples formed one big explosive tidal wave. I squeezed my mouth tight to stifle a scream.

I fell on my back and puffed loudly. "Oh. My. God. Orlando."

He looked pleased with himself as he wiped my release from his mouth with the back of his hand.

"You're not meant to be that good." I panted.

"Why?"

"I've been with guys much older who haven't a clue. They actually hurt me when they visit down there."

"Down there?" he laughed. "Your cunt. Your pussy. You mean?"

"Yeah. My cunt." I looked at him and somehow saying it made me throb for his dick.

"Let's just say I like hanging out with older, assertive chicks."

"They trained you well," I said.

Sliding down, I placed his dick inside my mouth. I licked, sucked, and teased until he was so big, I nearly gagged. His blissfully tormented groans inspired me to return the favor and devour him.

He touched my head. "I want to fuck you." His eyelids were heavy with arousal. Under the moonlight, his face expressed that hungry need I'd seen under the lamplight when we were together in bed.

I opened my legs and placed the head of his pulsating cock against my slit. As he slid in, the burn made my eyes roll back. I groaned all the way as he filled me to bursting point.

"I love your dick."

"And I love your pussy. Tight, wet, and supple."

"Supple?" I asked, looking at his grinning face.

"Like all off you."

He thrust in deeply and then withdrew before reentering teasingly slow, almost to the point of agony. He radared in on my G-spot and electrified me with a scorching wave.

He spun me on top. My breasts fell into his mouth as I bounced over his wet cock.

With his hands on my hips, he directed me as we moved as two voracious sex-starved strangers might. Only we weren't strangers.

His thrusts accelerated until the intensity of the friction between us combusted.

His jaw clenched, and a tormented groan damped my ear. As his climax gushed inside of me, I surrendered and left my body, dancing amongst the stars that I'd been admiring all night.

Holding each other, we lay in silence. My face rested on his firm chest. Wrapped in his strong arms, I felt blissfully sated in that memorable moment, witnessed by the moon and the dark velvet sky.

16

ORLANDO

Zane was so enthusiastic about my songs, he advised me to employ a manager.

I sat in Jake Stein's ultra-slick office, staring at signed, framed photos of famous rap artists and R&B performers he'd managed.

"What's your ambition, Orlando?" He sat forward, and his overpowering cologne wafted up my nose.

I opened my hands. "To play music."

He laughed. "Okay. Let me rephrase that. Where do you want to see yourself in five years?"

"Playing music. Surfing. Um…" Having wild sex. I kept that to myself.

"Girls?" he asked, raising an eyebrow. "You're a promoter's dream come true, Orlando."

I sniffed. "I like girls, if that's what you mean."

"Pity."

I studied him and noticed a little hint of arousal in his gaze.

"I'm not gay."

"Oh, well, not everyone's perfect," he said, almost to himself.

I considered myself broad-minded, but I didn't like being hit on by guys.

"Is that going to be an issue?" I asked.

"Are you kidding?" He jerked his head back. "I'm just playing with you." He rubbed his hands together. "Image. We need to set up a photoshoot. Surfing, you say?"

"Yeah… Well…" My shoulders tensed. I hated talking about my accident. "I was paralyzed for six months and only just got back on my feet three months ago."

His eyebrows met. "That sounds like a fucking nightmare. But hey, you've come good. Well done. That shows grit and determination."

"I had a lot of support. A nurse helped me get my head out of my ass, so to speak."

"You move well. You're great on stage. Although I'd like to see you perform the material from your album. I love jazz like the next guy, but it's not going to make me rich. Your album, however, is gold. You're like a new John Mayer."

I nodded sheepishly.

"You don't like him?"

"Yeah. I do. But I'd like to be known for my own style."

He grinned. "Oh, I love you young talented artists. I've got news for you. It's all been done before."

"So?"

He studied me a long while. "I like you. You're a little cocky. But you've got more fucking talent in your little finger than half of the artists on my books combined. I want you."

"Okay." Although he bordered on patronizing, Jake's kick-ass attitude was a shot in the arm. Direction wasn't my strong point.

If I had it my way, I'd make music, hang at the beach, and fuck Harriet.

"So, are you ready to hit the big time?" he asked, rubbing his hands together.

"Depends on what I'm expected to do. Photos, sure. But I don't want a ton of paparazzi up my ass 24/7."

His eyes gleamed as he chuckled.

"I want to turn you into a brand. But something tells me you'll revolt." He tilted his head as if trying to see me better.

"Yep. You got that right. Just book me into smallish venues. Keep it real. I'm more than happy to play the game. But no morning shows or shit like that. I want to be respected by music-loving people, not housewives."

"Housewives are powerful money-making machines." He studied me for a moment. "But hey... I get you. You're a Thornhill. You're already filthy rich, so you're not in this for the dough."

"That's right. I just want to get my music out there and enjoyed."

"Soon as I heard the album, I loved it. I particularly like 'Crash'. That's a great song. Strong lyrics and a catchy riff."

"That's my favorite, too." Expressing my recent struggles, that song meant everything to me.

"What are you up to tomorrow night?" he asked.

"Not much. I might go and play some jazz. Why?"

"I'm hosting a party at my place in Beverly Hills. There'll be lots of influential folk. Do you feel like playing a couple of tunes from your album?"

I shrugged. "Sure. I'll have to see what the guys are doing."

"You can play on your own, too, can't you?"

"With this material, I can. But I prefer the ensemble."

"Of course. The more the merrier." Passing me a card, he added, "Give the events manager a call, and let her know what you might need."

"Sounds good. It will be our first ever public gig. Other than the family shows." I smiled.

He studied me for a moment. "That's right, you're part of the wealthy Malibu scene. My God, if you let me, I can make you a star."

I shrugged. "I just want to get my music out there. That's all."

"Modest, too." He shook his head. "You really are a dream come true."

I rose. "We'll see you tomorrow, then."

"We're going to do good." He nodded.

After leaving Jake's office, I headed back to Venice, tossing up whether to drop in on Harriet along the way.

Deciding against it, I'd already visited every night that week, I didn't want to give her the wrong impression, despite my craving her.

The next night, we drove up to Jake's large state-of-the-art home. Resembling a glass cube and reflecting the turquoise twilight and surrounding cacti garden, it looked surreal.

Kelly, the events manager, met us at the door, and after shaking my hand, words spilled out of her at lightning speed. My assumption that she'd had some blow confirmed after she offered me a line of coke.

With Miles and Allegra standing close, I declined. Even if they weren't there, I was off everything. Just beer and the odd joint. I needed to get my shit together. The accident had changed me. I was no longer that boy who didn't do consequences.

After staring life squarely in the face, I'd decided that I could extract all of my pleasure from music and women.

I followed Kelly from one room, filled with knickknacks and wall-to- wall windows, to another.

"Will this work for you?" asked Kelly, pointing to a corner of a large space that opened out to the terrace and pool area, where all the guests gathered.

I nodded. "We just need electricity, and we're set."

She nodded. "There's plenty of food in there, and do help yourself to drinks. The servers are getting around." She pointed at a burgundy room filled with minimalist art and abstract sculpture.

"We should be good from here," I said.

"If there's anything you want, be sure to let me know." She smiled and left.

People milled about, talking loudly and laughing. Despite being early evening, there were guests everywhere. Lots of pretty girls wearing little. Some bounced about in the pool, literally. There were older dudes in their designer slacks and bright-colored shirts, and the odd eccentric wearing loud, androgenous outfits. I'd seen them all before. I'd been to so many parties like it.

Steve set up his standup bass alongside Alex's drums. Miles plugged in his electric keyboard, and after I'd tuned my guitar, we were ready.

We headed over to the food table for a quick bite before starting.

Allegra picked at the offerings, looking for vegan options since she'd joined Miles in his decision to stop eating animals.

"Do you think this is vegan?" She sniffed at her plate.

I shook my head. "You're serious?"

"You bet. I love animals."

"Well, so do I," I said. "But I'm still okay eating steak."

A man in a floral blazer, standing close, overheard and turned to face Allegra. "The vegan stuff's over there." He pointed at a table. "I'm familiar with this caterer, and they always put on a delicious spread. It's always the first to go."

Allegra gestured to Miles, and they both headed over to the table with an array of colorful offerings.

Opting for a burger, I grabbed a beer from the bar and found an empty table in the garden.

The magic subdued light of twilight, when day crossed into night, always gave me a buzz.

I'd only been there a few minutes, chomping into my meal, when two girls came and joined me.

"Hey," said a pretty blonde girl with a bright smile. "Do you mind if we join you?"

I shook my head. Despite not being in the chatty mood, I didn't wish to appear rude.

"I'm Danielle, and this is Sarah." She pointed to her friend.

Sarah's dark, unsmiling eyes burrowed into mine as though she was trying to read my soul. Normally girls with her kind of witchy features intrigued me, but Sarah chilled my spine.

"So, are you a friend of Jake's?" Danielle asked.

"He's my new manager."

Her blue eyes sparkled with curiosity. "Oh, are you an actor?"

"No. I'm a musician."

Sarah stared at me without blinking. "What do you play?"

"I like jazz. But I've just released a new album that's more R&B."

"You're Orlando Thornhill, aren't you?" Sara asked.

"Uh-huh." How she knew me, I couldn't say. But I wasn't about to ask.

"So what's the name of the album. Can we download it?" Danielle asked.

"Picture This."

"Really? That's so cool," she sang, switching from me to her serious friend for an endorsement.

Sarah stared down at her phone. "Here it is." She handed her phone to her friend.

"What an interesting cover," Danielle said. "An empty frame with a question mark."

I sniffed. "That came late one night. After a few too many."

"I like it," said Danielle.

"What's your star sign?" Sara penetrated me with her eagle stare again.

"Pisces," I replied.

"Creative," she said.

"I try to be."

"And a dreamer," she added.

She got that right.

"And into fantasies and very sexual," she continued.

I couldn't argue with that, but I wasn't about to encourage her. The two girls were like day and night. While Danielle's sunny smile seemed permanent, Sarah's mouth drew into a straight line.

I rose. "Nice meeting you both. I better get back. We're playing here tonight."

"Wow. Can't wait," Danielle said with stars in her eyes.

I left them and sensed Sarah's unshifting stare burning a hole into my neck. Did she know something I didn't know about myself?

17

HARRIET

After dropping Ava off at my parents' and fielding a barrage of questions about my health from my mother after I rejected a slice of my favorite cream pie, I headed back downtown.

Why hadn't Orlando called? And more disturbingly, why did I need to hear that raspy, clit-teasing voice to make my day?

My chest tightened on learning of his gig at a Beverly Hills party. Visualizing flirty girls flouncing about in tiny bikinis, I wondered if he'd revert to being a player.

Orlando had mentioned he no longer wanted to be that wild guy, while clutching my ass and insisting I straddle his face so that he could lick the hell out of me.

But was all that toe-curling pleasure worth a torn, jealous muscle?

As it was, I was on my way to meeting Jackson for dinner. And although the thought of food made me want to throw up, I accepted. More to get back at Orlando for going to a party full of glamorous babes.

Having only just turned twenty-one, Orlando would naturally fuck around. If only my heart stopped shriveling into a pea whenever I visualized him with another girl.

I pushed Orlando away from my thoughts and finally parked my car.

Although Jackson had offered to pick me up, I suggested we meet instead. As I entered the trendy Italian restaurant, I saw him seated in the corner, smiling at the waitress who'd just set down a bottle of wine.

He lifted his chin. "Ah… there you are. I was starting to think you'd stood me up."

I plonked myself down. "Sorry." I tilted my head.

His purple shirt's top buttons were undone, revealing hints of a buff chest. With that permanent five-o'clock shadow and chiseled jawline, Jackson exhibited the type of rugged masculinity I normally went for. Were it not for Orlando, Jackson would've made my pulse race.

After a bit of small talk, the waiter delivered our meals.

Bile raced up my throat as soon as the rich, garlicky aroma billowed toward me.

I ended up drawing circles on my plate with my fork while Jackson talked endlessly about himself and his latest exhibition.

"I found my own place today," he concluded, taking a sip of wine and wiping his lips with a napkin. He pointed at my plate. "You don't like it?"

"I'm not that hungry. But it was nice," I lied.

Having missed my period, I froze at the thought of a pregnancy test. I kept telling myself a stomach bug was to blame.

On the odd occasion I managed to speak, Jackson's glazed eyes would wander about the room.

At least Orlando was a respectful listener.

After dinner, we found ourselves on the busy strip with people crowding the sidewalk.

Jackson turned to face me. "Would you like to come and see my new pad?"

I shrugged. "Okay. Is it far from here?"

"Nope. Just up the road." He pointed at the congested Sunset Boulevard. Cars sounded everywhere. People yelled. Police sirens rang. A typical Saturday night.

"You're in the thick of it," I said.

"I like being surrounded by noise. It reminds me that I'm alive."

I had to smile at that. "I'm the same."

We arrived at a cutting-edge glass-fronted building with face recognition for entry.

"Mm... this is fancy," I said, following him into the marble-floored entrance.

"I'm now selling to collectors, and a gallery in New York wants a show. Things are looking good. Even with alimony." He grinned.

As we rode the elevator, he inched closed. His shoulder rubbed against mine and he gazed down at my breasts.

My mind swam in so many directions. On one hand, fucking Jackson might stem my Orlando craving. Or on the other, which was how it felt, he might make me desire Orlando more. As if that were possible, considering how invested my heart already was.

Why did it feel like cheating?

Orlando had made it clear we were casual lovers. When asking him if that meant fucking others, I read his shrugged response as a "Yes".

"I've only just moved in," Jackson said, turning on a lamp.

I stepped around the unpacked boxes and did a quick sweep of the huge open-floor space. The white, empty walls and lack of decoration made the speckled lights and strips of sky reflecting off the ceiling-to-floor windows the central focus.

He rubbed his hands together. "Can I get you anything?"

"Just water, thanks," I said.

"You're not drinking?" He sounded disappointed.

"Why, do you want to take advantage of me?" I asked.

He smirked and his eyes turned sultry. "I've wanted to take advantage of you from the moment I met you."

I lowered myself onto the leather sofa. Was I really about to do this?

I had to move on. Orlando was recreation. If only I could convince my heart.

Jackson returned with my water and a bottle of beer.

He leaned against a shelf while studying me.

"You mentioned you have a five-year-old," he said.

I nodded.

"And the father?"

"The father, as far as I've heard, is still a cheating asshole." I pulled a tight smile. "I don't give a shit about him. And Ava's the best thing that's happened to me."

"Yeah. Kids are great."

"And what about yours?" I asked.

"I've got two. A boy and a girl. Cassie and Cole. They're such free spirits. You know? No bullshit, like us adults." He chuckled.

I couldn't disagree, thinking of Ava and her endless impromptu dance performances. "Responsibility helps keep it real. We don't get so self-absorbed, I suppose."

"Sandy, that's my ex, is making it fucking hard," he said, staring out the window. "She's punishing me by not letting me see the kids as often I'd like."

"Oh... I'm sorry," I said.

He came and joined me on the couch. "Enough of my shit. We're here. I'm rich. You're beautiful. And life's great."

His eyes darkened again and before my next breath, he'd drawn me into his chest, and his lips crushed mine.

They aren't Orlando's, my body whined. I had to unclench muscles around my lips to allow his slobbering tongue control.

After he squeezed my breast, I shrugged out of his hold. "Ouch."

"You've got great tits," he said, his breath heavy. His stubble scraped at my cheek as his face remained close.

His hand slid up my thigh, hooking into my panties.

It troubled me that I wasn't aroused. Everything felt wrong. His smell. His rough fingers. No tenderness. I loved hard, hot sex, but at that moment, my emotions pined for tenderness. A warm breath on my cheek. A gentle nibbling of my ear or neck. Just like Orlando always did before getting dirty and wild.

I wiggled out of Jackson's arms. "Look... Um..." I adjusted my blouse and smoothed down my skirt. "I'm not feeling it. Sorry."

His eyes narrowed, and his lips flattened.

What had I seen in him?

"You're cock-teasing me," he said.

"I didn't promise you anything." My spine stiffened, and I stepped away. "I've still got feelings for someone else."

"Oh, the boy." He smirked. "He's probably out fucking some pretty young thing. He's rich. What are you expecting?"

I wanted to punch that smug look off his face.

I turned away, collected my bag, and hurried to the door. "Thanks for the dinner."

He followed me and grabbed hold of me. "Don't go. Let's just sleep together. I won't force you to do anything."

"It's not a good idea, Jackson," I said, yanking my arm away.

"Women throw themselves at me all the time, you realize?"

"Then call one of them," I said, turning the doorknob.

He clasped my wrist, and with his other hand pushed the door shut.

"I want to fuck you." He pushed me roughly against the wall and clawed at my breasts.

He was a big man, and he placed his weight against me. I regretted wearing a dress as he ripped at my panties.

"No!" I yelled. I tried to fight him off, but he was too strong. He undid his zipper and pulled out his dick.

"See how hard you've made me," he said.

He placed the head between my folds. Although he had a small dick, it still hurt.

His steamy breath dampened my cheek as he thrust in deeply.

"Oh, you feel nice."

I wanted to puke. And as he thrust into me, I was so overcome with repulsion, I kneed him in the balls and shoved him away with enough force to shift a car.

I ran for the door. "If you follow me, I'll scream."

He stopped at the door and then slammed it.

Lucky for me, the elevator was there waiting. I jumped in and leaned against the cold metal wall, tears streaming down my face.

18

ORLANDO

"Crash" received a thunderous applause from the hundred or so guests at the party. Having arrived at my darkest hour, that song had come from a deep place. Flying from my pen in such a burst, the lyrics resembled scrawl.

The song was a powerful reminder of how meaningful the things that I'd once taken for granted had become, like swimming in the ocean, climbing cliffs, or dancing under the stars with a girl in my arms.

Jake sauntered over and flashed a toothy smile. "You're going to be a star. Look at the girls. And the boys."

"It felt good performing to a new audience. It's nice to experience enthusiastic support from someone other than family. Thanks for the invite."

"The pleasure's all mine," he said. "You're going to stay and party, I hope?"

"Why not?" I smiled.

I headed over to Miles and Allegra. As usual, a line of men surrounded my sister, chatting her up.

Miles looked at me and rolled his eyes.

I laughed. "Don't worry. Allegra's only got eyes for you."

"You sang well. Your voice keeps improving. And they seemed to like the material."

"Good, yeah?" I clipped my guitar case down. "Are you sticking around?"

He consulted Allegra, and she shook her head.

"I might stay for a bit," I said. "I'll load my stuff in the car so you can take it home, if that's okay."

"Sure. Have a good time. You earned it," Miles said, patting me on the back.

After I packed my equipment into the SUV, I waved them off, and headed back into the party, and joined Steve and Alex.

"Are you staying?" I asked them.

With their eyes popping out of their heads, while ogling the topless girls bobbing about in the pool, they returned a simultaneous nod.

"My God, look at her. Are those real?"

I looked at the breasty blonde and laughed. "Maybe."

"Dude, how can you remain so cool?"

"These parties all look the same after a while," I said.

They turned toward me in unison, shaking their heads in disbelief.

"I'm fucking dreaming. Don't wake me," Alex said.

"I'm not as titillated," I said as a smile stretched my face.

Laughing, Alex said, "There's plenty of titillating going on here tonight. Holy fuck." His focus followed a couple of girls bouncing around in the pool.

I'd seen it all before and, while I enjoyed staring at naked breasts like any hot-blooded male, I wasn't as turned on as them.

I couldn't help but compare these women with Harriet. It was deeper than just my former nurse's hot body. She'd seen the dark side of my soul. She got me.

These feelings messed with my head. I wasn't ready for a committed relationship. I needed to find myself first. All the things that once mattered now seemed meaningless.

As I wasn't driving, I decided to hang around and have a few drinks.

I headed over to a table of food in the dining room, when a bunch of girls followed me in and gathered around me, firing questions at me, while I munched on chips.

They followed me to the pool area where girls and guys splashed about while others lulled about on floating seats sipping cocktails.

Jake joined me and crooked his finger. I followed him into a room that looked like a study with wooden bookshelves and an antique desk, where a handful of people sat around sharing lines of coke.

"Can I offer you a line?" he asked.

Sarah stood close. Her penetrating eyes zoned in on me again.

"She likes you," Jake said. "Everyone does."

"They don't know me."

His brow contracted as he studied me. "We'll arrange a photoshoot. Get you out there. Speaking of which..." He gestured at someone holding a phone aimed at me.

Jake stood next to me and placed his arm around me. "Smile. These will be the party's official snaps."

"And the unofficial ones?"

"They're the money shots."

"The money shots?"

"You know the sleazy, suggestive ones. They happen later. Stick around."

"No, thanks. I'm not in the mood for a scandal."

"A little bit of scandal here and there never hurt. Look at Kim. One sex tape, and she became a star overnight."

"That won't be me. Sorry to disappoint," I said.

"Pity. Are you religious?" he asked.

"Nope. But I've recently had an epiphany."

His face scrunched as if I'd admitted to joining a cult. "For someone so young? That's midlife crisis shit."

"I've always been mature for my age." I grinned. "Let's just call it a quarter-life crisis. In any case, it feels like I aged twenty years in the past six months."

"You don't look a day over twenty-five," he retorted with a chuckle.

I smiled. Harriet would be pleased to know I looked her age. Even though she didn't feel or look older than me. Our age difference only worried her. Not me.

Sarah joined us. Her eagle stare zeroed in on me again. "Did I hear that word epiphany?"

I took a deep breath. Was I really in the mood to share? "Up to about six months ago I partied pretty hard, but after my accident I'm seeing things differently."

"Don't go all religious and clean on me just yet." Jake chuckled. "You have the makings of a stellar career. Nothing like a little wild bad boy for that gold to turn platinum." He looked at Sarah, and she nodded.

I shrugged. "I'd like the music to do the talking."

"As I'm sure it will."

A young guy sauntered over and placed his arm around Jake's waist.

"This is Eddy. Eddy, this is Orlando."

I took his soft hand, and he returned a soft smile.

After passing on a line of coke, I left the room and headed back to the snack table. My appetite had increased since walking again.

Sarah followed me out. "Come and have a drink," she said. "There's a great punch. One of my special party brews."

Considering she reminded me of a witch, I almost laughed. "A brew?"

She nodded, and her lips moved up at one end. It was the warmest she'd been. For some reason, she kind of fascinated me. And at least she didn't have an overexcitable, screechy voice like some of the others there.

She led me to the large punch bowl, poured a scoop of pink liquid into two glasses, and passed one to me.

It was strong but with a fruity flavor. "Mm... let me guess. Gin?"

She nodded. "Among other ingredients."

I should have questioned her on that, but taken by the strong liquor and sweet fruity combination, I gulped it down in three mouthfuls.

"Have another," she said.

I studied her teasing dark eyes. "Are you trying to get me drunk?"

She shrugged. "Why not have a good time? Sounds like you could use it."

"I'm good now," I said.

"I can see that. But from what you were saying earlier, I sense you've been taking life pretty seriously. It doesn't harm to let your hair down every now and then."

"Hey, you're talking to someone who's spent the last five years partying hard. This scene's tame compared to some of the shit we got up to."

"This party's only just warming up." She arched a thick black eyebrow.

Hip hop blared from the speakers and people milled about yelling over each other, while waiters moved about with trays of snacks and drinks.

After three glasses of punch, I decided to settle for the more sensible choice of beer.

A woozy sensation hit me. Euphoric lightness glided me along. The punch had more than liquor in it, which shouldn't have surprised me. Sarah had referred to it as a brew after all.

A couple of topless girls stepped out of the pool and came up to me. They placed their wet arms around me while someone aimed their phone and took a photo.

"Hey, no way," I said, freeing myself from their grasp.

They giggled. "Don't worry, we'll just keep it for ourselves."

I predicted that it would be plastered all over social media any minute.

One of the girls tried to unbutton my shirt, but I grabbed her wrist and shook my head.

Her plumped lips turned down. "Most of the boys have taken their shirts off, and it's such a warm night."

I turned to Sarah. "What was in that punch?"

"Ecstasy and Ayahuasca."

"You're fucking kidding me?" All of the sudden the shimmering turquoise pool turned kaleidoscopic.

My body felt like rubber and I laughed at anything and everything. I removed my shirt and dived into the pool. It was like being in a warm bath, as I floated on my back peering up at stars cascading over me.

I felt a hand reach into my briefs. My dick was hard. Not due to anyone in particular, but because of the blissfully warm high.

"Oh… you feel nice." A young, feminine guy ran his tongue over his lips.

Waking out of my drugged haze, I shoved him away. "Fuck off," I snapped, snarling at him. My fists were positioned to knock him out.

Sarah stood between us. "Leave him alone. He's hetero."

"Pity. He's hung like a horse."

Now I knew how women felt when groped by strangers and jerks.

I jumped out of the pool, and Sarah tossed me a towel.

"Come inside," she said, helping me gather my clothes. "I'll make you a coffee."

Wearing a towel, I followed her in among cat calls from some girls.

That was the last thing I remembered, before finding myself naked in a bedroom.

I'd lost a big chunk of time. It was night outside.

Golden-framed portraits on the teal walls showed distorted faces that warped in animation. The freakshow a product of my own tripped-out making.

Heavy sighs and moans drew my attention to the king-size bed, where Sarah sucked on a girl's tits while fingering her.

I closed my eyes, and a warm mouth moved up and down my dick. My head fell back. I thought it was Harriet and even called out her name. But the girl didn't possess Harriet's artful lips.

As I surrendered, I imagined Harriet's tits bouncing as my cock rammed into her. I blew in someone's mouth and then fell back on the chair and laughed.

By the morning, I woke on the bed with Sarah and another girl. I sprang up and scrambled about for my clothes.

Sarah sat up and said, "Breakfast?"

I shook my head. She acted as though we were a couple who'd just spent more than a debauched night together.

I massaged my face. "I'm not sure what I did last night after…"

"After Sally blew you, you crashed."

I was relieved that it was only a blow job. Although Harriet and I were casual, I still felt like a cheat, even if I hadn't initiated anything.

"I can hardly remember a fucking thing," I said. "How the fuck did I get here?"

She laughed. "Willingly."

Just as I stepped into my apartment, I received a call from Jake. "That was great last night. I heard you made quite a show of yourself."

"Sarah gave me a few glasses of punch." My head was fuzzy and my tongue furry as I gulped down water.

"Shit. One glass would have been enough," he said.

"I should have been warned. I'm seriously pissed off."

"You looked like you were having a good time."

"I was fucking molested in the pool," I said.

"Yes, I heard about Sammy. Sorry."

"He's lucky I don't press charges. I'm tempted to."

"Come on. It was a bit of fun," he sang.

"That's bullshit. I felt fucking sick. I still feel violated." I fell onto the sofa. "Look, Jake, I'm moving on. I want a management team that doesn't want to turn me into the next new sex scandal."

"That's not the game with us. But sex does sell. And you're fucking hot. The girls and boys are going to love you."

"I don't want that. I'm moving on."

"Wait," he said. "Okay. We'll stick to nice shots of you on the beach. That kind of thing. And we'll make a video of the band. I'll bring in a top crew. The best. You'll shine," he said.

"Mm… Let me think about it. I'm still raw and shitty at the moment."

"Hey, I'm sorry about the drugs. I thought you knew about the punch. Look, let me speak to Sammy and Sarah. Expect an apology by the end of the day."

I took a deep breath. "I want nothing to do with them. I don't want them knowing my number. Just get my music out there without the drug-fueled orgies. The music will do the talking. Got that?"

"Loud and clear. We'll speak soon."

I stepped onto the balcony where the hot late morning sun seared onto my bare torso.

After I changed into my shorts, I headed over the road to the beach. The sand squelched on my feet as I sucked back the salty air and dropped my towel.

I virtually fell into the sea. The cool water, splashing on my face, revived me. I almost felt normal again.

Even though I hadn't looked at my surfboard since the accident, I'd now started to body surf, and as I caught a frothy wave, I soared along, knowing one day soon I'd jump on my board again.

19

HARRIET

Ava sat on the bed, braiding her doll's hair while waiting patiently for me to rise. I couldn't face the day. Nausea churned in my belly. I kept seeing Jackson's sweaty face rubbing against mine. What had I seen in him?

I forced my heavy body up.

"Mommy." Ava pointed at my bruised wrist.

"I fell over. It's nothing, darling."

Just as the horror of the night before revolved in my head, the buzzer sounded.

"Go and see who that is, sweetie," I said. Without a moment to spare, I bolted to the bathroom and puked.

"Mommy, are you okay?" Ava asked, standing by the door.

"I'm totally good." I rose from the floor. "I just ate something bad last night."

"Again?" she said, shaking her head.

I smiled sadly as I passed her. "Who was that?"

A knock came to the door just as she said, "Ollie."

Before I could respond, she ran to let him in.

Ava liked Orlando. He always bought her sweets and little gifts, and he treated her like family.

That placed me in an awkward position since she saw him as a buddy and had no reason to suspect that Orlando and I had crossed that line from friends to lovers.

I threw on a T-shirt and leggings and washed my face. I looked a wreck. One of the advantages of being around each other every day was that Orlando had seen me without makeup. He'd even said he preferred me that way.

"Hey," I saluted, entering the living room.

"I tried calling. You weren't picking up," he said, looking bronzed and sexy, even if a little tired.

"Oh... I slept in," I said.

He set a box on the table. "Donuts." He looked at Ava. "There's some with chocolate, too."

Her little face lit up.

"That's kind of you," I said. "I'll make some coffee." I turned to Ava. "Go and watch television, and I'll bring you a glass of milk and some donuts. Okay?"

She nodded with a big smile, went over to the TV, and turned on some cartoons.

Orlando followed me into the kitchen, which was separate from the living area.

His gaze traveled over my body, making my nipples tighten. I wasn't wearing a bra, and I could almost smell his arousal. But in the rush to change, I'd forgotten about my naked arms.

He pointed at my bruises. "What happened?"

Searching for the right words, I bit my lip.

"What happened?" He persisted.

"Um... a guy tried to grab me."

His brow contracted sharply. "Where? Do you know him?"

My feet became a blur as I stared down with tears burning my eyes.

"Who was it?" he asked.

"Shh…" I tipped my head toward the other room.

He stood close. So close I could smell the sea, his maleness, and I turned to putty.

"Tell me," he demanded.

I poured coffee into two cups and remained silent.

"Was it that douche from the gallery?" he asked.

Opening the box of donuts, I set two on a plate, poured a glass of milk, and took it out to Ava, who bless her soul, was lost in her own world watching TV. "Here, sweetie." I bent down and kissed her. "Love you."

"I love you, too, Mommy."

Tears threatened to pour out. The lump in my throat made it hard to speak. I turned quickly away.

I gestured for Orlando to follow me into the bedroom.

We entered my untidy room with my underwear strewn about. "Excuse the mess."

His brow remained furrowed.

I sat on the bed and drank my coffee. He joined me. His arm rubbed against my shoulder and my body tingled.

"Who was it, Harry?" he asked.

"It was Jackson. I guess it was my fault," I said, unconvinced, but I had to quash Orlando's sudden intensity.

"It's never your fault or any other woman's, for that matter." He turned to face me and held my hand. Staring down at my wrists, he shook his head. "He's not going to get away with this."

"No. Please. Don't. He's likely to cause trouble for the Artefactory. He has a lot of influence in the art scene. Leave it."

"Did he go all the way?" he asked.

I bit my lip, nearly drawing blood. I couldn't tell him, so I lied. "No. I kneed him in the balls and ran."

His mouth twitched into a faint smile before straightening again. "Good on you. But shit, look at you." He looked at my marks. "He fucking hurt you. The fucking asshole."

His hand remained in mine, and his eyes shone with concern. The longer he gazed, the deeper he chiseled into my soul.

I couldn't take it anymore; I fell into his arms and sobbed, pouring out anxiety, repulsion, and guilt for having gone to that asshole's apartment in the first place.

I unraveled from his arms, and he handed me the box of tissues by the side of my bed.

"I'm really okay," I said, brushing back my hair. "I'm a mess, and I need a shower. I only just got out of bed."

"Sorry to come barging in like this." He held onto my hand. "I'm glad I did. Because you wouldn't have told me otherwise."

I stared down at my feet and nodded.

"Look, Harry." He tipped my face up to meet his gaze. "You can always tell me anything. I want you to know that. You're my closest friend."

I looked into his eyes and was met by another man. He was older suddenly. The pain from the past six months showed on his face. Or was he trying to tell me something?

"But you've got Miles and a ton of drinking buddies," I said.

"I don't share with anyone what I share with you."

My throat lumped up again as he stroked my cheek.

"I'm going to knock that bastard's teeth out."

"No. Forget it. Please," I said. I got off the bed and picked up my clothes. "I should have a shower." I paused for a moment. "Why did you come here?"

"I came to see if you wanted to do lunch."

"I've been invited to Miranda's. Ava's dying to get over there. She misses Malibu." I smiled tightly. "So do I."

"I miss you," he said, looking at me seriously again.

"And I miss you," I said, turning away because tears kept falling.

He stepped closer and touched my shoulder. His breath pricked my neck, and I turned around.

As our lips touched, I swallowed back emotion, extracting willpower from his warmth.

We separated and stared into each other's eyes and shared a tender smile.

"Okay, I might invite myself to lunch, then," he said.

"I'm sure they won't mind. You and Lachlan are pretty tight."

"Sure are. I look up to him as an older brother."

Orlando watched cartoons with Ava while I showered and dressed. It was so sweet seeing him there giggling as Sylvester chased Tweety, reminding me of the boy he still was. Even though naked, he was a hot-blooded man.

Being a perfect beach day, we decided to have a picnic by the sea. The children made sandcastles while we swam and sunbathed. Miranda, Lachlan, and Manuel joined us, and we made a day of it. It was fun and helped take my mind off things.

"I miss my home," Orlando said as we ambled along the shore.

"Why don't you move back?" I asked.

He stopped and stared into my eyes. Something weighed heavily on him. I'd seen that same troubled look in his eyes before. "Because I want to keep seeing you." He took my hand. "And I need a private life."

"We are seeing each other. Like now," I said with a trembly grin. I'd never been this emotional before.

"No. I mean. Let's be open about it."

"Oh. You mean tell Ava about us?"

He nodded slowly. "If you're okay with that."

My jaw dropped. That, I wasn't expecting. "But you're young and starting a career. The girls…"

"I can still have a career and see you, can't I?"

"Let's see what happens in the next month or so."

Was I pregnant? Should I tell him now?

So many thoughts raged; I couldn't think straight.

He met my eyes with a question. "But I want to be with you. Like now," he said, drawing me into his hard chest.

Leading me by the hand, he brought us to a secluded spot, hidden by rocks. And we lowered onto the sand.

"I want you. I think about you all the time," he said.

His lips were all over mine.

I pulled away. "What about if your parents see us?"

"No one comes to this spot. I've been coming here for years."

A smile touched his lips.

"Ah…" I knitted my fingers. "Your love den."

"Please don't, Harry,"

I frowned. "Don't what?"

"Judge me by my wild days," he said.

"I'm not." I opened my hands.

He took me into his arms again, and I felt his arousal thickening against my stomach. As he tightened his embrace, I flinched. My arm ached where Jackson had grabbed me.

Loosening his hold, he said, "I'm sorry." He studied my bruise. "That fucking douche is going to pay for this."

His eyes darkened again. With that buff body, I could imagine Orlando capable of holding his own in a brawl. Only that was the last thing I wanted.

His lips trailed up my neck and settled on my mouth. I felt his hunger and need as he held me against his body. I nuzzled into his warm neck and breathed in his salty masculine scent. Heat flushed through me. My nipples tightened and an aching need to be filled throbbed between my legs.

We lay on the sand, and he rubbed my erect nipples.

He pulled back the small triangle of my bikini. "I loved perving on you in the water, bouncing around with those eye-popping nipples all hard and teasy."

I giggled. "Teasy?"

As I indulged in the warmth of his tongue, searing desire ate away at me.

He parted my legs, and his fingers traveled up my thighs. My heart pumped wildly all the way to my core.

Using soft feathery touches, he teased my clit. I widened my thighs, ravenous for all of him.

"I need to eat your pussy." His rasp slithered over my puckering flesh.

A battle brewed inside of me. Torn between hunger and fear. We could easily be discovered. But all it took was a glance at his simmering dark eyes for my brain to shut down.

Clawing into his shoulders, I had to bite my lips to stifle a scream as he devoured me. His tongue lapped over my pulsating bud. As one tingling ripple after another turned into a tsunami. Swept away, I succumbed to hot pleasure.

Hooking my fingers into his shorts, I reached in for his velvety, hard dick. The smooth head moistened my palm.

"Ahh... I need to... fuck you," he stammered.

He entered me in one deep thrust. His arms bulged as he positioned himself on top of me.

The burning stretch made my eyes roll back. My appetite had been whetted by his tongue, and now I wanted to be turned into a shattering mess.

"I love being inside you. You feel hot," he said. His hands smothered my breasts, and his hips rocked against mine.

As he filled me, his lips sucked on my neck.

A surrendering sigh left my lips. His thick length rubbed against the G-spots I hadn't felt before Orlando. My eyelids fluttered, and my legs tensed.

I thought I would combust from the need to release as he plowed into me, tantalizing nerve endings, and setting off spasms as my convulsing sex clung on for the ride.

"I love you, Harry." His words caressed my ear. The sensation of his breath traveled down between my legs and hurled me over the edge. I fell from a steep height, and became a soaring bird catching a warm, breezy current.

He continued to fuck me, moving like a tiger chasing his prey. His heart pounding in rhythm with mine.

His dick spasmed, and he blew so intensely, he trembled in my arms.

We fell onto our backs and laughed.

"That was kind of dangerous," I said, panting. "We could have been spotted."

"I don't care," he said.

Sand speckled his jawline, which I brushed away. His contagious grin curled onto my lips. That moment and us was all that mattered.

He lifted me up in his arms. "Come on, let's have a dip to wash off the sand."

Carrying me in his strong arms, he laughed as I wiggled about yelling, "Don't! Put me down!"

Tossing me into the water, he became a boy again. I splashed him in protest.

From hot and steamy to playful, I was in love, and everything, battles and all, suddenly made sense.

20

ORLANDO

My new song became a hit virtually overnight. Suddenly everyone wanted a piece of me. I had endless requests for interviews and television appearances. I would've preferred to just play gigs. But as Jake kept reminding me, promotion was essential if I wanted to reach people.

I called Harriet. "Hey, sexy."

"Hey. How was the interview?"

"Just like all the others. A studio audience of screaming women."

"You're showing off again," she said.

"Not really. They were all older than my mom. Hey, how do I get face paint off?"

"What they painted you up like a clown?" she asked with a chuckle.

"Almost. Television makeup. Water doesn't work."

"No. You need some good old-fashioned makeup remover."

"More like paint stripper." I laughed. "Can we catch up later?"

"Sure," she said. "Ava's at my mom's house. I'm here alone tonight."

"Catch you soon, wearing nothing, I hope," I said.

She giggled. "I'll see what I can do."

I headed back to the penthouse for a nap. It had been an early call. All I seemed to do was go from one interview to another. We weren't making much music, which weighed heavily on me.

Just as I stepped into my apartment, my phone buzzed. I ignored it, but it kept ringing so I picked up.

"I've been trying to call you for the last hour," Jake said.

"What's up?" I asked.

"There's a tape getting about," he said.

"What sort of tape?" I asked.

"Of you having your dick sucked," he said.

"What?" I frowned. It wouldn't be the first. I had a few of those back in my last year of college. And one of the reasons why I dropped out. "From my past, you mean. We paid those off."

If I could rewind and edit my seedy past, I would. While my mom cried over my decision to leave college without a degree, my dad threatened to knock someone's teeth out if the tapes weren't destroyed. In the end, he used his checkbook and not his fists.

"The tapes are from the party with Sarah and her blonde friend in starring roles."

"Oh, fuck," I said.

"Hell dude, you've got quite an asset there." He chuckled.

"Fuck you and your sleazy scene. This isn't a fucking laughing matter."

"Sorry, Orlando. But to be honest, it doesn't show you in a bad light."

"If I wanted to be a porn star, maybe. Where is it?"

"I've sent it to you. I've had it removed. But it will appear again somewhere."

"Give me Sarah's number?" I asked, my heart racing. This was the last thing I needed.

"I'll text it to you. I thought she would have given it to you, since you were all chummy at the party."

"That was her being all chummy. I should press charges. She drugged me, the bitch."

"Hey, it was a party. Shit happens," he said.

"Fix it." I tossed my phone and yelled, "Fuck."

Within an hour, a few of my old party pals called. They'd seen the tape and wanted to be part of the scene again.

"Ollie's back," Aaron yelled down the phone.

"I've never been gone, you fucker. You guys bailed on me as soon as I was paralyzed. Go fuck yourself."

Unable to bring myself to watch the tape, I called my dad.

"Hey, Ollie," he said, with that deep paternal tone that brought a lump to my throat. I'd done it again. Let the family down. And this time it wasn't completely my fault. Just naïve me thinking the best of everyone.

"Dad. I need to see you. Can we talk?"

"Sure. I'm downtown right now. I can be there in half an hour," he said.

"That would great. I'll be here waiting," I said. There was a pause. I wanted to tell him I loved him, but my throat was too thick.

The only time I cried, other than after the death of my first dog, Rocket, was after the accident and since then I'd remained raw. I wanted to be that easy-going dude who strutted through life. I pined for that version of me, minus the fuckups.

It was late afternoon when my dad arrived. I let him in and we hugged.

"It's been a while since I've been here," he said, looking around the large open space. "You've kept it pretty clean."

I almost laughed at his surprised tone.

"I'm a tidy freak. Always have been," I said, forgetting to mention my cleaner who came daily.

"You take after your mom in that area." He fell onto the leather sofa.

"Can I get you get something?" I asked.

He shook his head. "I'm good. I just had a long lunch with an old army buddy."

"You're not driving, I hope," I said.

"No. I've got James downstairs." My father studied me for a moment. "I've heard your new song. We all have. It's everywhere. We're proud of you. It's a great song. I liked it straight away. That's always a good sign. It's got a great melody. Beats a lot of the stuff out there. If you can't hum a tune, then it stinks."

I had to smile. We'd had this discussion often. My dad was old-fashioned in his tastes. Tastes that had rubbed off on me.

Studying my father, who could still make a room of women gush, I wondered if he'd had his share of scandal when he was my age. I got the feeling there'd been a few problems. But they'd never come up. Only my grandfather's wild days garnered the most attention when reflecting on the wild 70s.

He sat with his arm around the sofa as I paced about. "What's up, Ollie?"

"I performed a few songs from the album at my new manager's party." I stared down at my hands. "I met this girl, and she gave me some punch."

"Shit. Not the punch," he said, stretching out his legs.

I rolled my eyes at how stupid that made me.

"Anyway, you drank from the punch bowl. Let me guess it was spiked?"

I nodded grimly. "I'll smoke a joint every now and then. But I don't do blow, and I stay away from pills. I've seen how crazy they can make people. And after the accident, I want to make a go of my life."

"That's good, son. And you will. You're seriously talented. You take after your mom."

"I thought I took after Granddad," I said. "He's the musician. And so are you, for that matter. A great one."

His mouth curled up at one end. "Thanks." He sat forward. "Tell me what happened?"

I told him about Sarah and the sex tape.

"Fucking technology." He shook his head. "In my day, that shit happened all the time, and no one ever found out."

I sighed with relief. I loved my dad for being open-minded and also forgiving.

"Please don't tell Mom."

He shook his head. "She could still hear about it somehow. The media's one big hellish rumor mill." He paused before asking, "Does Harriet know?"

That gave me a start. I didn't even think he knew about Harriet and me. "Um... No." I bit my lip and looked up at him tentatively. "You know about Harriet?"

"Your mother told me. It's pretty obvious you like her."

"Mom doesn't approve?"

"Your mother's going to be hard to please. No one's going to be good enough for you, save an Ivy League scholar with a doctorate in art or a concert pianist." He laughed and made me smile at how idealistic my mother could be.

"I haven't told Harriet. We're dating. But that's it. No plans. I'm young. I want to focus on my career. But I like seeing her. She's good to me. And she's not spoiled, rich, and entitled, who's more interested in having her nails done than developing this." I tapped my head.

He sniffed. "That's what drew me to your mother. Her love of art and not herself. I mean, she wasn't insecure about herself. She had an inner strength I liked. Full of dignity and a beautiful heart."

His eyes softened as I'd seen time and time again when talking about my mother.

"What am I going to do?" I asked, rubbing my neck.

"Give me the source, and I'll get the checkbook out," he said.

I nodded pensively. "Sorry, Dad."

He stood up and joined me at the window as we watched the parade of eccentrics along the boardwalk.

Chuckling, he pointed to a chubby man prancing about in a polka dot G-string. "The crazies are still here. Good to see."

I laughed. I was blessed. I had the greatest dad on the planet.

We looked at each other and smiled. I hugged him. "Love you, Dad."

21

HARRIET

Soon as I saw Jackson, my legs turned to concrete and my heart pounded. He'd come by to organize the packing of his art. I should have left it to Clint, but it was my job to be there.

I'd arrived a nervous wreck. My gentle but insistent work buddy didn't miss much. I told him how Jackson had tried to rape me. It hurt to talk about it. Ugly memories were like an unflushable turd they kept returning to haunt me.

He shook his head in disgust. Just as Orlando had suggested, to whom I hadn't gone into as much detail with, Clint insisted I press charges.

Orlando had even offered to pay for the lawyer and to support me, which choked me up. I was still processing that "I love you" he'd uttered on the beach.

In any case, the last thing I needed was a court hearing. I couldn't drag my daughter into that ugly scene. How would she feel knowing her mother had been raped? It was best left alone. A friend of mine had taken an asshole to court and ended up in years of therapy. The defense successfully argued that she'd led her assailant on.

I couldn't risk that happening to me. Jackson had the cunning and the money. And that town was teeming with crafty lawyers.

"I can't even look at him," Clint said, entering the kitchen where I'd gone to hide.

I shrugged. "Maybe I shouldn't have told you. It's put you in a sticky situation."

"No." He touched my hand, and his blue eyes shone with concern. "I'm always here for you. Remember that."

We hugged, and a tear slid down my cheek.

"You stay here, lovey," he said with a soothing tone. "Let me sort everything."

As he marched off, I hardly recognized my normally bouncy colleague.

Channeling Clint's steely courage, I sucked it up and headed out to the gallery.

I found him pointing at Jackson, who'd arrived with two friends. "You're lucky Harry hasn't called the cops, yet."

Jackson looked over Clint's shoulder at me with a blood-curdling smirk.

How could I have liked that jerk?

"I don't know what kind of lies she's spreading. She's probably pissed off because she's not my type." He almost pushed Clint out of the way as he strode off.

Clamping my jaw, I gnashed my teeth and charged after him.

I blocked his way. "If I'm not your type, why the fuck did you leave bruises all over my arms?"

As we stood in the alleyway, I returned his sneer. "I should have you arrested."

He stood virtually on top of me. His face was close to mine. "Do your fucking best. You've got nothing on me. You're just a fucking cock-teaser. And you can stick your trendy, little hipster gallery up your tight ass."

He pushed me, and I stumbled onto the ground, landing on my butt.

I opened my mouth to scream when I found myself up in the air.

Orlando pulled me up. "Are you okay?"

I was too dazed to speak.

Where did he come from?

The next few minutes stretched like a distorted hallucination.

Orlando had Jackson by the scruff of his neck and pinned the older man against the wall. He jabbed his finger into the artist's sweaty face. "You're a fucking rapist. A small man with a small brain that lives between your balls."

Before I could intervene, Jackson shoved him off. Orlando's veins tensed in his neck.

Jackson didn't stand a chance. Orlando threw punches as though hitting a swinging bag. Bone-crunching blows echoed in the alleyway, as Jackson fell onto the ground clutching his stomach.

Although it might have been seconds, it felt longer. I finally found my voice, screaming, "Stop!"

Clint and Jackson's friends came running out, and the two men jumped in, pulling Orlando off Jackson.

Straining out of their hold, Orlando looked flushed. His eyes wide and coated in rage. He shoved them off and followed me back into the gallery.

"Are you okay?" I asked.

He nodded, wiping his mouth with the back of his hand.

"Come into the bathroom," I said, leading him along.

I left Orlando to clean himself up and headed back out where I found Clint alone in the gallery.

"Where are they?"

"They've gone," he said, shaking his head. "That was fucking intense. Jackson asked for it." He looked up at the walls. "At least they got what they came for. We won't need to deal with him again. And to be honest, I hated his work. I can't imagine why it's popular."

"The gallery made a packet, though."

He puffed. "Yeah. It did. But still."

I turned and looked at Orlando. His scratched face, and wide, almost black eyes reminded me of a maimed, wild animal. A beautiful one.

Watching him rub his bruised knuckles, I said, "I better get you some ice for those hands."

"Don't worry. I'm good." Orlando smiled tightly and turning to Clint said, "Sorry you had to see that. He pushed Harry onto the ground."

"He's a fucking savage. Thank god, his show's over."

I passed Orlando a glass of water.

Clint looked at me. "I wish you'd call the police."

Ignoring that plea, I focused on Orlando instead. "Maybe we should go to hospital. You took a few blows."

"Pussy punches. Nothing to worry about." He grew a few inches, as though to prove that point. Before me stood a strong, powerful man.

I touched my colleague's arm. "Let's forget this ever happened. Okay?"

He shrugged. "If that's what you want."

I left him and stepped into the office.

"Where the hell did you learn to fight like that?" I asked, as Orlando followed me in.

"School. Bars. You know boys."

"I'm surprised to see you." I was actually stunned. He'd never dropped into the gallery before.

"I was in the area and thought I'd pop down to see your beautiful face." He took me into his arms. "And I'm fucking glad I did."

All it took was a whiff of him, and my hormones stirred. All the drama faded away as his lips caressed mine.

Pulling away, I studied him. The only time I'd witnessed that troubled glint in his eyes was while he lay in hospital.

"Is there something wrong?"

"No." He rubbed his lips together. "I just felt like seeing you."

I could only put his edginess down to that fight.

"When do you finish?" he asked.

"I am just about to leave. I'm going to Malibu. Miranda's invited me and Ava for the weekend."

"I'm staying at my parents' for the weekend. I need a surf."

"Oh," I responded, a little jittery. I'd bought a pregnancy test so that Miranda could hold my hand during that moment of truth.

Orlando took me into his arms again and held me. "I'm really into you, Harry." He kissed my neck, and I melted.

"I'm going now," Clint called out.

I released myself from Orlando and went to the door. "Sure. Have a good weekend."

"I will. I need a break," he said. "And so do you." He smiled sweetly. "Will you be okay to lock up?"

"Sure." I smiled and watched him sashay off.

I returned to Orlando and let him ravage me on the sofa.

I sat in Miranda's huge bedroom. We were alone. Lachlan was surfing, and Sherry had taken the children to the beach.

Instead of freaking out over my impending test, I kept visiting the lust in Orlando's eyes from our last steamy encounter when my gripping nails nearly ripped a hole in the sofa.

We'd reached a new place. Even though the sex between us was driven, there was also tenderness. Orlando's soothing touch helped me forget all about Jackson's brutality.

Three minutes lasted forever. That dreaded line formed, and I puffed a stuttered breath.

I was pregnant. *Hell.*

Miranda patted my hand.

"I knew it." I shook my head. "Fuck."

"You're going to have to tell him," she said.

"I know. Unless…"

That ugly question smacked me in the face. I wasn't ready for two children as a single mother.

Reading my mind, Miranda frowned. "You can't. I'll help you." She stretched out her arms. "I've got all of this now."

"And you've got the gallery to run. And I love being there. It's given me a new lease on life." I sighed. "Even if I hate some of the pretentious douches that come with it."

Miranda smiled sadly. "You're doing really well there. You fit in. And you've always been better at math than me. We almost don't need an accountant because of you."

"Thanks." I took another breath. "Fuck." I held my head. "I finally get something happening in my life…"

Miranda rose and cleared away the plastic wrappers. "I thought you were on the pill."

"I must have forgotten to take it." I twisted my mouth.

"You must be around eight weeks."

Staring down at my hands, I nodded. "What am I going to do?"

Miranda placed her hands on her hips. "You're going to have it. And you'll tell Orlando. I mean, he's fucking rich, for God's sake. He'll be able to pay for a nanny. And we'll be here. This is Ava's second home. We love her being here. The more kids, the merrier. Lachlan loves kids."

I thought about how sweet Orlando was around Ava. And how he always clowned around with Manuel. "Yeah. Orlando's pretty good around kids." I rose and paced about. "But he's only just launched his career. I can't expect him to settle down with me. And then there's Clarissa. Hell…"

"What about Clarissa? She's a lovely woman."

"She is. But I don't think she likes me being with her son."

"I don't think it's you personally. She's a protective mother. And maybe she was trying to protect you. He was a serious player, you know."

Mm… was?

My sister was making a lot of sense, but that knot in my gut just got tighter.

22

ORLANDO

I ran back to shore and joined Lachlan. Untying his strap, he asked, "How did that feel?"

"It felt fucking great. I'm back," I sang, high on endorphins.

I couldn't contain the grin. My mojo had returned. Being able to stand on that board and soar again felt like nothing else.

Ava squealed with laughter as Manuel buried her in the sand. It brought back memories of when I was a kid with me doing just that with Allegra.

I watched on and laughed. Manuel ran around in circles like some kind of wild kiddy ritual.

"I don't get the allure of being buried myself," Lachlan said, going over to the children. He shoveled off the sand and helped Ava out.

"Now, it's your turn," she said to Manuel, who was creating a sculpture of feathers, seaweed, and rocks.

"Perfect swell. Not too fast or furious," Lachlan said, pointing at the waves.

"Yeah. I would've thought those waves boring once." I rolled my eyes at my former daredevil stunts.

"You'll get back to that."

I shook my head. "No fucking way. This will be me from now on. Bigger is no longer better."

He rubbed cream onto his arms. "That sounds wise. It's good to see you back, though."

"Thanks." I exhaled. "There's some drama happening."

We plonked ourselves down on our towels.

"What's happened?" Lachlan grabbed a bottle of water from his backpack and a couple of apples.

I took the apple he offered me. "Thanks."

Lachlan munched away as he listened to me recounting the events of the party.

"You should sue, man. That's shit. Drugging you like that."

"I've been there a ton of times before. I used to look for the spiked punch." I sniffed. "But blackmailing me through a sex tape? That's fucking low."

"What does this Sarah want?"

"She wants to hang out."

"And she'll release the tape if you don't?"

"She already has. My manager and a few others have seen it. She's now threatening to send it to Harry."

"Bring in the cops," he said.

"When I warned her. She just laughed it off." I shook my head. "I don't want to lose Harry."

"Harriet's been around. She'll get over it," he said.

"I guess so. I like her. A lot," I admitted, watching the kids splashing in the shallows. "I tried to move on. I even tried to hook up with Chloe."

"Tried?" His head jerked back.

"Well… We didn't get very far. There was no chemistry." I drew a circle in the sand.

"What happened to the girl-a-night dude?"

"I'm no longer that guy." I pulled a crooked smile. "Even if I had felt something, Chloe's a virgin." I shrugged. "I've never been with one before. It comes with a lot of responsibility."

Lachlan nodded thoughtfully. "I've only been with one, and I married her." He chuckled. "And I'm happier than I've ever been. I couldn't imagine my life without Miranda."

"You're great together. And I like being with Harry. It's just that a tour's about to happen."

"That's wonderful." He patted my shoulder. "I've heard your latest tune. It's a good one. A classic."

"Dad said something along those lines. Even my grandfather likes it."

"That's saying something. Grant's pretty fussy. He's never made it past the 70s."

"No. I think his influence has rubbed off on me." I took a breath. "What should I do about Sarah?"

"Press charges. She's stalking you."

"Do you think Harry will understand?"

He nodded. "She's a grown-up."

"I really like her. A lot."

"She really likes you, too. Are you sure you're ready to go all the way?"

I puffed a slow breath. "All the way? Marriage, you mean?"

"You're still pretty young and with a career unfolding."

I rubbed my neck. "That's the thing. I love Harry. But I'm not ready to settle down and marry. I've suggested we go exclusive and see where it goes."

"Then play it by ear. I'm sure she gets that you need to sell your music. Do tours."

I picked up my surfboard.

"You'll figure it out, I'm sure." He patted me on the back.

Lachlan gave me the push I needed. I'd been burying myself in my music and between Harriet's thighs, but it was time I spoke to Sarah.

When I returned to the house, I went straight upstairs to my room and called her.

She picked up straight away. "Orlando."

"You've got to stop stalking me."

"I'm not stalking you. You just don't return my calls."

"That was a pretty fucking low act, sending that video out."

"It's sure to help your career," she said.

"I don't need that kind of fucking help."

"Why don't we meet and talk about it?" she asked.

"Only if you promise to delete those files."

"Why don't we meet at the Rainbow Café."

I couldn't believe she knew that place. It was a tiny café close to the studio where I'd been recording.

"Okay. I can be there in an hour." I closed the call abruptly.

I tried calling Harriet, but she didn't pick up, so I left a text to say I'd be there later.

We'd spent every night together that week. She seemed a bit distant at times, which I put down to that asshole Jackson. I'd held her hand and asked her if she was all right and if she wanted to talk about it. But she shook it off and brightened up instead.

I sensed Harriet didn't like unloading, which on one hand, I understood, but on the other, I needed her to know I was there if and when she needed to talk, scream, or cry. In the same way that, as a nurse, she'd been there for me. Even after I'd acted like a first-class jerk.

When I arrived, I found Sarah scrolling through her phone. It was the first time I'd seen her since the party and planned to make it my last.

She looked up. "Hey." As usual, her lips barely moved. I even wondered if she was suffering from depression because she was the most serious person I'd ever met.

I ordered a soda and asked, "Do you want anything?"

"No. I'm good."

Looking into her heavily kohled eyes, I said, "What do you want?"

"Some cash would be good." She remained straight-faced.

"You're blackmailing me?"

"You're rich. You can afford it."

I thought about my father with his check-book opened, waiting to hear from me. But her demands still pissed me off.

I shook my head. "Who the fuck are you?"

"I'm a model and an actress. And I need some money."

"So, you set me up?"

"No. I didn't. We were smashed. It was nice. Wasn't it?" She tilted her head.

"I can barely fucking remember. I never consented to it. Least of all, for a fucking amateur porno."

"One can make a lot of cash from those."

I leaned forward and stared square into her face. "I want the fucking thing deleted. I didn't come here to catch-up."

Her brow puckered. "That's antisocial of you."

"How much do you want?"

"One million should do it," she said, staring at her sharp black-painted nails.

"That's a bit fucking steep."

"It is what it is."

"What's to stop me from going to the cops?"

"Oh, you don't want to do that."

"But it's already out there," I said. "What more can you do?"

"I've removed it for now."

I'd had enough of staring at those menacing eyes and rose.

"I'm reporting you to the cops."

Sarah smirked. "You better not. I know about your girl at the Artefactory."

"Have you had people following me around?"

"Nope. I just know lots of people. This is a small town when it comes to our kind of crowd."

"You're not my kind of crowd."

"I know lots about you, Orlando Thornhill. You're famous. And there are other sex tapes, I'm told. It's pretty hard not to meet some chick whose heart you haven't crushed."

I shook my head. "I never promised anyone anything. Everyone knew the score. That was before my accident, when I was still partying hard."

"I know." She smirked. "Lots of orgies. I've watched a few. You're insatiable."

I exhaled a breath. My wicked past had finally caught up with me. It wasn't so much the damage to my reputation, but the pain it would inflict on my mother and Harry.

"If I get you that cash, will all this end?"

She nodded.

"You'll need to sign something legally binding."

"Sure."

I stared at her for a moment. "I thought those tapes were meant to be destroyed." I recalled my father paying a large sum to have them removed.

Sarah scrolled down her phone and clicked on the screen before passing it to me. "Here's one."

I watched the hazy scene of me fucking a girl doggy-style. I couldn't even remember seeing that one. I wanted to vomit. "Where did you get that?"

"Oh… there are a few getting around. What do you expect? You're rich and hot. And everyone's got a phone handy." She raised an eyebrow. "I'm not from money like you. And this town's tough. I need to survive."

"I get that. But why not something honest?"

"Honest?" She laughed. "Waitressing doesn't cut it. And I need bigger tits for porn. That's what the money's for."

I'd had enough of her face, which grew uglier by the minute. I left her alone with her sly smirk as I headed over to Harriet's, stopping at a florist along the way.

23

HARRIET

Orlando seemed distracted, which didn't help my own state of mind on whether to reveal my pregnancy. I settled on remaining quiet for now.

"What's the matter?" I'd lost count of how many times I'd asked that.

"Nothing," he said abrasively.

"It doesn't feel like nothing."

Rising from the bed, he rubbed his neck. He'd arrived at Miranda's late when everybody had gone to sleep.

One of the many advantages of the large property was I always stayed at the back away from everyone, which meant we could have noisy sex.

That night, however, we'd fucked as though we were both hiding something.

His tongue lashed at my pussy roughly, tipping me over the edge of reason. As if driven by a dark force, he made my nerve endings spark and tingle. When it came to fucking, Orlando had honed a seasoned player's instinct.

That's what ate at me. Not just his devouring tongue and dick, but also the fact that he was young with a bright future.

How the hell could he commit to a relationship?

I threw myself into my work, putting together a budget. While Miranda's talents lay in curating sell-out shows, she sucked at math. Whereas I loved numbers. Especially when the figures tallied in profit. I loved seeing Miranda's eyes widen with glee. The gallery was a success, which meant my job was safe.

She'd just brought in a new artist who'd flown in from New York. Stefan Sanson was much older and quieter than some artists we'd worked with. Miranda asked me to sit in on their meeting, which I appreciated.

As we saw him out, Miranda whispered excitedly that his work had sold out everywhere, and that we'd hit a home run having him there.

We returned to her office and celebrated with a donut and coffee.

"You haven't spoken about what you're going to do," Miranda said, putting her feet up on her desk.

"That's because I haven't decided." I bit into a fingernail.

"But Ollie's leaving soon. Aren't you going to tell him?"

"He's already left. He's about to tour the UK and Europe. He'll be gone for at least six months. I can't upset his plans."

"That's for him to decide."

"I don't know what to do." I paced about. "I'm almost three months."

"I'll help you." Miranda looked me in the eye. "You've got to have it."

"Women terminate every day. It's our right. The world's overpopulated, anyway. It's not going to miss one extra baby, is it?"

She packed her laptop into her bag and rose. "Harry, I know you. Remember, you said the same thing while expecting Ava. Could you live without her?"

My shoulders slumped as I puffed out. My darling daughter was my universe.

"You should have told him. You still can. Write to him, for god's sake."

My nails dug into my palm. "You didn't see what I fucking saw. He had his dick sucked while we were seeing each other. It made me realize that he's just a boy who's not ready to be a father."

"You saw a sex tape?"

I nodded slowly. "He's released that catchy tune. It's going through the roof. I see his photo everywhere. It's killing me. I've even stopped looking at social media."

Miranda frowned. "Shit. That's tough." She looked at me. "Why didn't you tell me?"

I flicked my hair back. "I don't know."

My dark, twisted side hated to admit how shitty my personal life was compared to her perfect marriage.

"I still think you should have told Orlando."

"Tell me, who makes good decisions when they're twenty-one?" I asked.

"I did," she said.

"That's you. You're sensible. And always have been. I'm talking about a seriously hot, talented young man with a bright future." I grabbed my bag. "I've got to go."

After we locked up and stepped out into the alleyway, I said, "Do me a favor."

"What's that?"

"Don't mention Orlando's name around me. I need a break from him. I need to start again. A clean page."

She hugged me. "Remember, I'm there to help. Mom and Dad will help for sure."

I hugged her. "Thanks."

ONE YEAR LATER…

My mother carried her legendary apple cream pie into the kitchen. "My, this place is huge."

A maid came toward her. "I can take that for you."

My father glanced over at a chef stirring a pot. "It smells delightful." He tapped his tummy. "I haven't eaten much in preparation for the feast."

I smiled at my excitable parents. Even my normally stoical mother struggled to wipe the smile from her face.

Miranda's baby's christening happened to coincide with Lachlan's birthday, and a big day of festivities had been planned.

We left the kitchen, and while my parents headed off for a walk through the gardens, I went in search of my sister.

I found Miranda in her room with her gorgeous daughter, Rosie, suckling on her breast.

"How is she?" I asked.

"She's good now."

Sherry knocked on the door and entered. "Um... Harriet. Dylan's needing a feed."

I followed her out and entered the nursery where my darling, chubby little dark-eyed baby cried. Apart from being a glutton, he was normally a quiet boy who slept most of the time.

Those past four months had flowed like a dream. Ava was in love with her new brother, as were my parents. Everyone around me had been so supportive I hadn't stopped smiling.

Dylan Thomas Flowers brought joy not just to me but also to my family. My mother, who'd suggested naming him after one of her favorite poets, held my hand all the way to when he arrived and stole our hearts. And while she continued to be pedantic about grammar, she was open-minded when it came to me being a single mother.

Grandchildren were all that mattered, she pronounced, watching as my dad bounced Dylan on his lap while pointing at the roaring lion on a David Attenborough documentary.

It had been an eventful few months. As a full-time employee of the Artefactory, I'd gotten the gallery's budget in order, therefore saving them a ton of money, while Miranda curated and discovered the next new thing in art. It worked well for both of us, and I sure as hell didn't miss nursing.

I'd just heard that Orlando had returned from his European tour. We'd seen him on television, and his music was everywhere. I was proud of him. And although I missed him like crazy, I'd trained my heart to stop clinging onto the hope of us being together.

Hot and spicy memories of our magical time together kept me warm at nights. Orlando would be a hard act to follow where new boyfriends were concerned, but I wasn't in any hurry to find love. Maybe I'd finally grown-up because for the first time in ages, I felt content within myself. Giving birth to Dylan had flushed away all my former angst.

The babies looked sweet together in the nursery. I looked at Miranda and shook my head. My heart was so swollen with love, I couldn't stop smiling.

"Two darling little cherubs. Cousins born a few weeks apart."

"Crazy, yeah?" Her eyes shone with concern. "Are you going to be okay about seeing Orlando? And you've already seen Clarissa."

While pushing my stroller into Juni's shop, Beautiful but Strange, to buy Dylan a cute pajama with mythical creatures, I'd run into Clarissa and she'd seen Dylan for the first time.

"You have to tell them," Miranda said.

I nodded with a sigh. "Clarissa suspects. You should have seen her face."

"Did she say anything?"

"Nope. But she looked like she was going to cry. It was shattering, and I couldn't talk. My brain crashed."

"That was yesterday. They'll be here soon. You'll have to tell them."

"So you keep saying. And I will. But here? I mean, it's a party," I said, biting my nails.

"Orlando dropped in yesterday to see Lachlan. He'll be here. He asked after you."

"You're kidding?" I shook my head in disbelief. "After traveling the world and becoming famous, he's still asking after little me?"

Miranda tipped her head and smiled. "You're not so little. You're stunning, sister of mine. And you have to tell him."

Sucking back some air, I nodded.

"Let's get out there and greet the guests," she said while checking on the baby monitors.

24

ORLANDO

My parents looked lost in conversation, wearing matching frowns.

"Hey. What's up?" I asked, joining them at the table.

"Have you caught up on sleep?" my dad asked.

"Yeah. I slept for ages."

"You look better," my mother said. "Lunch should be ready soon. And then there's the party next door. Rosie Peace's christening."

I nodded. "I met her yesterday. She's beautiful. Lachlan's over the moon. He couldn't stop carrying her around and making silly voices."

My dad looked at my mom and smiled. "Yep, that was me with Allegra and you."

My mother remained with a long face.

"What's the matter?" I asked.

"Harriet's had a baby."

I nearly dropped the bottle of water in my hand. "Huh?"

She nodded. "I saw him. He's named Dylan. He's beautiful. And he looks exactly like you did as a newborn." Tears trickled down her cheeks, and my father took her hand.

"Clarissa, it's too soon to tell. It's only a few months old."

"A few months old?" I said almost to myself. That would mean that she was with the father twelve months ago. Blood drained from my face as I sat down heavily. "Shit."

"Were you together, then?" my dad asked.

I nodded slowly.

"Exclusive?"

I looked at my dad and shrugged. "We never really talked about it." That was bullshit, but our relationship had been too deep and personal to share with my folks.

Harriet had remained in my thoughts throughout my tour. Even after all the girls I'd partied with while abroad. None of them were Harriet.

Puffing out a loud breath, I said, "Look, it might not even be mine."

"Why wouldn't she tell you?" my mother asked.

"Knowing Harriet, she probably didn't want to stand in the way of my tour."

"That makes sense, I suppose," my father said, knitting his brows. "And look, we could be assuming too much here. Let's just wait and see what happens."

I nodded. "That's the right thing for sure. Thanks for telling me. It won't come as a big shock today when we see her."

My mother hugged me. "It's so nice to have you back. We missed you. And you've done so well."

Nodding in agreement, my father added, "The album's great. Even Grant's crazy about it."

I smiled. "I thought of him when I created it."

"I can tell," he said.

After I left my parents, I headed over to the Chalmer's. I wanted to see my sister and also catch up with Miles.

Although I'd begged Miles to tour with us, he'd been too deeply invested in his studies to commit to a tour. Despite being a talented musician, astronomy had become his primary focus.

I found Miles's dad polishing his car in the driveway.

"Hey, Sam. Love the color," I said, admiring the turquoise Mustang.

"I've just had it repainted. Juni picked it. She's crazy about loud colors." He laughed.

"I've noticed." I thought of his wife and those attention-grabbing outfits she favored.

"Are you going to Lachlan and Miranda's christening?" he asked.

"Sure am," I said. "See you there. I'm just going over to see Miles and my sister."

"Congrats on the album. We listen to it all the time."

"Thanks for the support." I saluted. "Catch you there."

I found Miles with his head buried in a science magazine as Allegra worked on fashion sketches.

"Ollie." Allegra hugged me. "I missed you yesterday. Mom said you'd crashed. I figured you needed the sleep."

"It's great to be back," I said.

Miles looked up at me with his warm brown eyes. "You must've loved Europe, though."

"It's mind-blowing. Like one big endless museum. I took a ton of photos. Everywhere I went, there was a picture."

"I bet," Allegra said. "I can't wait to go." She looked at Miles, and he nodded.

"You'll have to go there for your honeymoon," I quipped.

They looked at each other and smiled in only that way that two people in love would.

"I'm so glad you're back. I've missed our little jams," Miles said.

"Me, too. I'm staying here at the house. I'm dying for a surf. Did you get the royalty check?"

"I did. Thanks. I mean, I didn't really do a lot."

"Bullshit. You came up with a legendary riff," I said.

"Thanks. It's a nice chunk of money, for sure," he said.

"So, you're a rockstar." Allegra giggled. "I've seen your ugly face everywhere."

"That's the worst part." I sighed. "All those silly television interviews."

"You come across as sharp," Miles added.

"That means a lot to know that. I thought I sounded like a dick."

"No, you didn't. You sounded good," Allegra said with a nod.

"Have you seen much of Harriet?" I asked.

"Not really. Occasionally on the beach with Miranda. That's all. Oh, and I went to an exhibition a few weeks ago at the Artefactory. That was fun." She looked at Miles. "It's such a great scene. It was more like a party."

"Is she seeing someone?" I asked. It wasn't the type of personal question I'd normally ask. But this was my sister, who I could talk about anything with. And Miles, despite being more interested in the rings of Jupiter than talking about girls, had always been that buddy I could confide in.

"I don't know," she said, looking at Miles. She bit her lip, and I could tell she knew something.

"I know that she's got a baby boy."

"Oh, you do?" She studied me closely.

"Mom and Dad just told me. Mom saw him in your mom's shop," I said, turning to Miles.

"Do you think it's yours?" Allegra asked.

"Mm… maybe." I played with my fingers nervously. My heart started to thump against my chest. It only just hit me; I could be a father. I looked up at my sister. "What if it is?"

"Then, I'm an aunt."

"Holy shit…" I said to myself. "Maybe she was seeing someone else. I wonder if she ever plans to tell me."

"She'll have to," Miles said. "I mean, she kind of should've by now."

I shook my head. "No. I get it. I know Harriet. She didn't want to stand in my way. That's her. She's the most unselfish person I've ever met. She always puts the needs of others before herself. And at the time…" I combed back my now shoulder-length hair. "I was being blackmailed with that sex tape."

"What happened to that?" Allegra asked.

"I paid her off. I haven't heard from her again. She was a drug user, so God only knows. I'm over that LA party scene."

"Good to hear." Allegra nodded.

"But you must have partied in London," Miles said.

"Oh, yeah. It was hard to avoid. Paris. London. Rome. One big endless party." I puffed a tired breath just thinking of the hangovers. "But you know, none of it compared to my life here."

A lovely bluebird settled in a tree, and I pointed. "There. Great timing. That little bird does more for me than any all-nighter."

"You've changed, brother of mine," Allegra said.

Yep. I'd changed all right.

I rose. "Best be off. I want a surf before heading to the party."

Allegra touched my hand. "I'm sure Harriet will tell you if you're the father."

I nodded pensively and left them.

25

HARRIET

The new dress I'd bought for the party fitted me snuggly. I adjusted the neckline so my exploding cleavage wasn't on show. Something hard to do since giving birth.

"You look great," Miranda said, standing by the mirror smoothing out her hair.

We'd shopped together and bought some new clothes, which proved a welcomed distraction from having to tell Orlando about Dylan.

I sensed Clarissa had probably already told him. There was no doubt in my mind that she knew. She'd gone so pale after seeing Dylan.

I prayed they'd forgive me for not telling them sooner. I hoped they'd understand why I kept it from Orlando.

As I studied myself in the mirror, I asked, "You don't think I look too fat?"

"You're perfect. You've finally got the big boobs you've been wanting all these years."

I laughed. "I know. They're as big as yours."

Her smile faded. "You're going to have to tell him. Today."

I nodded slowly, gritting my teeth.

Miranda took my hand. "He'll understand."

"Maybe I should have told him sooner." I sighed. "But this is his moment. And look at what he's become. He's probably got stunning women everywhere. I couldn't stand it. My jealousy levels would have peaked. And knowing Orlando, he would have stuck by me."

"Don't overthink it, sweetie. And he asked after you."

"He would. He's a good guy."

She brushed a lone strand off my face. "Your hair's grown so long. And I love the purple streak. Blonde suits you. You look gorgeous, Harry."

"And so do you, Andie."

We shared a giggle.

The day was perfect. Sunny and warm and with just enough breeze to make it comfortable.

Lachlan, wearing a permanent smile, held onto Rose as though she was the most precious thing in the world.

When the Thornhills arrived, I fumbled about, driven by a bundle of nerves. I'd just given Dylan his bottle that I'd expressed so I could enjoy the odd drink. Milk spilled everywhere as my hand trembled.

Through the window, I caught sight of Clarissa smiling and chatting to Lachlan with Aidan by her side. His arm was around her. Their unwavering love for each other, always so endearingly on display, validated that notion of "happily ever after."

My mother entered the room and as I cradled Dylan, said, "He's such a good baby." She opened her arms. "Here, let me hold him."

I passed my chubby little boy over to her. She tickled his belly and as he giggled, our world lit up.

She wore a sympathetic smile. "Don't worry, love. I'm sure they'll understand."

We'd moved into the dining area when Clarissa and Aidan joined us. They saw Dylan on my mother's lap and their focus remained glued on my son. Clarissa held onto Aidan's arm as though she might faint.

"Howdy," Aidan greeted us before returning his attention to Dylan.

"Um, this is my mother, Jane." I turned to my mother. "This is Clarissa and Aidan Thornhill, Orlando's parents."

Holding my dozing son, my mom rose.

The pair remained transfixed as though they'd seen a vision or something spiritual.

Clarissa's eyes misted over. "He's so beautiful," she said with a quavering lilt.

"Would you like to hold him?" my mother asked.

She nodded.

Aidan, whose focus remained glued on Dylan, appeared stunned.

"He's such a big boy," Clarissa said. "Nice big cheeks."

"He was nine pounds," I said.

"Really?" She glanced at Aidan. "That's how much Orlando weighed."

We huddled together admiring Dylan when Orlando waltzed in.

His eyes found mine and lingered. Everything blurred. It was just the two of us.

Orlando's wavy hair had grown, and his stubble accentuated those lips that had tasted every inch of me. But it was those dark chocolate eyes that held me in a trance. They spoke to me of his struggles and lust for adventure. Although he looked older, he was still bone-meltingly beautiful.

"Welcome back," I said, finally find my voice.

"It's good to be back. I missed everyone." His gaze trapped mine again.

Tension not only had me by the throat but made time freeze, and the air thickened between us. Barely able to breathe, I craved space to clear my head and calm my racing heart.

As Clarissa placed Dylan in my arms, her eyes met mine and instead of justifiable resentment, she showered me with warmth, discharging the trapped air from my lungs.

She said, "We'll leave you to it."

As Orlando's attention went to his son, Clarissa took his hand, and Aidan gave him a subtle nod.

It was time for *that* talk.

I gulped to steady my nerves. "Why don't you get a drink, Orlando."

He nodded. "I think I need one."

I set Dylan in his crib, sat down, and took a steadying sip of wine.

Orlando returned within a few minutes holding a bottle of beer.

I waited for him to pull up a chair, before asking, "When did you return?"

"Yesterday morning. I slept all day." His attention returned to our son. "Dylan's a great name."

I smiled. "Dylan Thomas Flowers." Pride sang off those words. I loved his name, and my mother for suggesting it. "He's named after a poet."

"My grandfather Julian would appreciate that," he said.

He stared into my eyes. "You look amazing. Beautiful."

"Thanks. I've stacked on weight."

"You're perfect." He took a gulp of beer and kept switching between me and Dylan.

Gaps of silence intensified the excruciating reality of that moment. "Look, Orlando… I know I should have told you. But…"

"You should have told me." His abrasive response, although bruising, was understandable.

I searched his face for signs of anger but was met with the same stunned bewilderment from his parents earlier.

He rose and went to his son, who slept peacefully and oblivious to the angst playing out around him. "He's beautiful."

"What would you have done?" I asked.

"I would have stayed and supported you." He wore the same steely expression I recognized from his former struggles.

"But what about your tour? Look at what you've achieved," I argued.

He shrugged. "So? I'm not as hungry for success as you might think. If anything, it exhausted me. I love the music, but I hate the circus that goes with it."

"You didn't enjoy your European tour?" I asked.

"I loved Europe. It's an amazing place. So much to learn and so different to here. But I love my home. I'm happiest when I'm by the sea. I love playing complicated music that doesn't appeal to everyone. The album's out. It's making a shitload of money. And now, I can get back to doing my own stuff."

"Then it's worked out well."

Dylan stirred, and we both started at the same time. Orlando followed me to the crib, and I lifted my baby and rocked him. My little boy's sleepy smile made my heart sing. At that moment, nothing else mattered but my beautiful baby.

"Can I hold him?" Orlando asked.

Seeing our little boy resting on Orlando's large bicep challenged my inner strength, as I fought back tears.

I wished I could capture that moment. If only for the tenderness reflecting off his eyes.

"He's so quiet." Orlando pulled a silly face, Dylan giggled, and my heart ached from love.

Tears streamed down my face, like I'd torn an artery of pumping emotion. All the months of bottled-in feelings poured out of me.

Orlando popped Dylan back in his crib, and his moist eyes met mine.

I fell into his arms, and he held me close, as friends sharing a life-changing experience might.

My muscles unwound and allowed his warm body to flood me with hope.

26

ORLANDO

Although I couldn't blame Harriet for holding back on what was the most important news I'd ever had in my life, my feelings were in a tangle. The shock of seeing my son for the first time left me speechless. My mind raced like mad, as did my heart.

But the longer I looked at my son, the calmer my mind became while my heart grew like the morning sun.

"Am I the last to know?" I asked, studying Harriet. With that waist-length hair and full figure, she'd blossomed into a gorgeous woman. She made all the girls I'd met overseas pale in comparison.

Biting her lip, Harriet frowned again. "Miranda and Lachlan know. My parents suspect, but they haven't really interrogated me." She stared into my eyes. "I hope you realize I don't expect anything from you."

"He's my son," I stressed. "I have a right to be involved."

Her face pinched. "Of course. As much as you want. But if you choose to pursue your career and leave for long periods, I'll understand, I don't expect you to drop your life."

"Drop my life?" I sniffed. "I dropped my life last year when I couldn't walk for six months. I've got no intention of wasting one more minute. And Dylan's part of my life. My story. Our story."

Her eyes widened. "*Our* story?"

I gulped back some air. "I love you, Harriet."

She frowned. "Orlando... you shouldn't feel obligated to say or do anything."

I shook my head. "I'm not just saying that because of Dylan." I paused for a sip. "I never stopped thinking about you. Why didn't you reply to my texts and emails?"

She exhaled loudly. "I wanted to. But I thought it best to give you space."

"Space? I had plenty of that. You could've written," I said.

"Why don't we join the others and have a nice day?" she asked, tilting her pretty head.

I grabbed her hand and drew her in close. "I meant it."

Her eyes seemed large as she scrutinized me. Before she could comment, our lips met, and I found a soft, inviting mouth. I drifted off to paradise. My body heated, and I wanted to devour her. I unraveled my hold instead. It wasn't the time to give into raging attraction.

"Have you gone off me?" I asked, unconvinced by the heat from her lips.

"No fucking way. I'm crazy about you." Her eyes reflected searing need mingled with uncertainty, or was that fear?

Although fear rang through me, I also felt excitement. Anticipation of something real and meaningful filling my world.

I glanced over at my sleeping son. He was a part of us. Born from love. A beautiful accident that suddenly I couldn't live without. That sentiment shot through me the moment he opened his sleepy eyes and smiled at me.

Harriet got me. She'd seen me at my worst. We'd shared so much during those months of my being trapped in a broken body. And the air between us seemed to spark.

"Motherhood suits you. You're sexier."

"I'm chubbier. And my tits have grown."

I stroked her cheek. "You look beautiful and healthy."

I turned to study my son, who looked so peaceful tucked in his blanket. "He seems like a quiet baby."

"He is an absolute angel. I'm blessed."

"We're blessed, you mean."

Watching her frown, I said, "I'm sensing doubt."

She knitted her fingers. "I've always loved you, Ollie. It's just that you're young, and one doesn't always make the right choices. And you're such a good person that maybe you feel you have to say these things."

"Say these things?" I shook my head. "You really don't know me. After everything?"

She seemed lost for words as she gazed up at me.

I took her into my arms, and our lips met for a slow, drugging kiss.

We separated and stared into each other's eyes.

"Come on, we should join the party. Sherry's here to keep an eye on Dylan, and I just fed him."

I held Harriet's hand, and we walked out of the room to mingle with the guests.

It was great to catch up with Lachlan, who held his little baby as a proud father.

"She's beautiful," I said, touching the baby's cheek.

"Isn't she?" Lachlan had that glow of joy that I understood suddenly, because something filled within me. It was inexplicable. But life suddenly felt complete. It was more than just discovering I had a son. It was also admitting to myself that Harriet was the woman I wanted to spend my life with.

Lachlan studied me for a moment, looking at me with delicate curiosity. "You've met Dylan?"

I nodded.

"Are you okay?" he asked.

"Sure. I mean, it's come as a shock. And I would have liked to have been told about him sooner."

"I figured that. I even tried to convince Harry. But she worried your career would be impacted and that you may regret it one day if you'd felt obligated to return."

"She told me that. And I suppose I understand where's she's coming from, but I still would've liked to have seen the birth of my child."

He returned a sympathetic nod. "Your album's great, though."

"I produced it here. I could have been at my son's birth and still made music."

"It's happened now. And well…"

"True. It's only starting to sink in." I shrugged. "Any way, I thought of Stevie Ray Vaughan and channeled the seventies when I made that album."

"I can hear it. That's why I really like it. It's earthy, and there's no gadgetry."

I laughed at his euphemism for digital overproduction.

"Mm… I made sure to stay away. We even used reel to reel."

"You don't say," he said, looking impressed.

"Mm… an eight track."

"Only an eight track?"

"It was good enough for The Beatles," I said with a chuckle.

"Too right."

"Although Zane, my producer, is no George Martin, he's still a whizz."

"It worked well. It's a great album. A classic. 'Crash' is a great song. We're hearing it everywhere. Even at the supermarket."

I pulled a face. "Hell."

He laughed. "That's what being successful is all about. Appealing to the masses."

"I suppose it's good to have my music enjoyed by more than just bearded dudes huddling over a bong."

Lachlan laughed. "Round Midnight misses you."

"I'm missing playing jazz. At the end of the day, I'm that musician."

He tapped me on the back. "You'll have to listen to my new boxset of Weather Report."

"Can't wait." We sank back our beers and laughed.

I watched Harriet in her figure-hugging skirt, swaying those hips gently as she walked, and firing up my libido as I watched her chatting and giggling with guests.

It was evening, and everyone was up dancing. Harriet moved her pelvis gracefully with her arms in the air. Those full breasts bounced slightly, and my dick grew harder by the minute.

I waited until she'd stepped off the dance floor and said, "Hey, how about a walk on the beach?" Pointing at the starlit sky and moon, I added, "It's a beautiful night."

She studied me for a long while, as she'd be doing all day. As though trying to read beneath the surface of my words. "Sure. Let me make sure Sherry's okay with Dylan."

I followed her in. I wanted to see my boy again.

When we entered the nursery, in the low lamplight that stamped fairies around the wall, the babies were sound asleep. I tilted my head and studied Dylan. He'd stolen my heart for sure. Every time I looked at him, warmth pumped through me.

I imagined taking him on walks along the reef when the tide was low. Just like my dad had done, igniting my love affair with the sea. I couldn't wait to share those simple pleasures that my soul still feasted on.

I wanted to kiss his chubby little cheek, but didn't wish to wake him. Instead, I stood there and indulged in an emotion I'd never experienced. My eyes burned as tears swelled. I sucked it back and left the room, feeling light. Dylan was the most precious gift I'd ever received.

As we headed down the track to the beach, I was reminded of the paradise that was my home.

"I've missed this," I said.

"It's gorgeous. I feel blessed having a sister living here. And now Dylan can also enjoy it."

"Our little boy won't want for anything," I said, taking her by the hand as we walked down the rocky steps to the beach.

27

HARRIET

It was like a dream. Orlando's hand fused into mine, and the energy emanating off our palms triggered a wave of desire through me.

We laid out a mat on the sand and sat down.

The moon reflected a pearly pathway along the dark ink sea.

"It's magical, isn't it?" Orlando said, turning to me. "I've missed you, Harry. I mean it."

My heart leaped. It was hard to fathom all this sudden outpouring of emotion. It was a different Orlando to the one I'd known. He'd grown up. He'd become a man.

"You do believe me?" he asked.

"You keep telling me, so I have to believe you."

The dark intensity of his gaze penetrated so deeply my soul recognized something real, and tears blurred my sight.

"It's just that…" I lost my train of thought as his fingers wandered up my waist and found themselves under my blouse. My nipples tightened.

As his hand gently moved over my bra, I winced.

"Too much?" he asked.

"I'm just really sensitive from breastfeeding."

He removed his hand.

I put it back. "I like it, though."

"You feel really nice, Harry."

I ran my hand over his big bulge. "And so do you."

He hissed behind his teeth. "My dick missed you."

I removed my hand. "But surely you've had lots of girls."

"Not that many. But it was like sport. And not deep. Not like what we have. I couldn't get you out of my mind. It made me realize just how strong my feelings are for you." He turned to face me. "You're not pissed off?"

"It's been a year, Ollie. I mean, I couldn't expect you to turn into a monk."

He laughed. "To be honest, I would have been better off reading a book."

I fell into his arms again, and it felt nice leaning against his chest and staring at the stars.

"Let's give it a go," he said.

"What do you mean by that?" I asked.

"Let's live together."

I looked into his eyes. "Really?"

"I'll buy a nice big house. Where ever you want."

I shook my head in disbelief. "You don't have to do this, Ollie."

"I really want to." He placed his arm around my waist and drew me in tight. "I mean it."

"But that's only because we have a son," I challenged.

"I never stopped thinking about you, Harry. In many ways, being apart for that time made me miss you more."

Under the moonlight, I could see sincerity shining from his almost black eyes.

Holding his gaze, I took a deep breath, and my lips touched his. Our bodies crushed as we laid down and made love. Right there on the beach. Our favorite place. Where I'm sure Dylan was conceived.

FIVE YEARS LATER...

"You're finally tying the knot," Miranda sang, braiding Rosie's golden hair. The beautiful child's big blue eyes shone with excitement. She was the spitting image of Lachlan.

Ava entered and showed me her latest costume—a polka dot, ruffled tulip skirt that looked like a flower when she spun around, kicking out the hem and revealing layers of contrasting ruffles.

She was now ten going onto eighteen. I couldn't believe how quickly she'd grown.

"That's looks amazing," Miranda said. "And now you're performing with the adults."

Ava nodded, looking pleased. She should. She'd won a prestigious scholarship into a performing arts school. "As is Mannie."

"Where is Manuel?" I asked.

"He's with Lachlan and Ollie, surfing."

"He better be careful, if he's going to pursue dance," I said.

"That's what I keep telling him," Ava said.

Dylan splashed about in the pool. "Look, Mommy." He did a somersault under the water.

I clapped and looked at Miranda. "He'll probably join the circus."

We laughed at Dylan's obsession with tumbling.

"Either that or take over the world."

"He is bossy. But he's good," I said, smiling at my beautiful dark-haired boy who was the spitting image of his dad. So much so that whenever Aidan and Clarissa were around him, they'd be close to tears for having another cheeky boy in their life. They showered Dylan with love and gifts, and Julian read him the classics. He was convinced that our son would one day write great poetry, just like his namesake, Dylan Thomas.

I didn't mind what my boy became, as long as he remained healthy and happy.

"We've been living together for five years and we figured it was time to do it properly." I patted my belly. "Especially with another on the way."

"What is it with us? We're ridiculously in synch." Laughed Miranda, who was also with child.

"Aren't we just." I chuckled.

The men returned with boards under their arms. Manuel had grown so tall that he now came up to Orlando's shoulder, and he was already a beautiful-looking boy. He always had been, but I could see he was going to melt girls' hearts.

I did wonder whether he and Ava would one day be together. They were really close. And they still partnered whenever Belen staged performances. They'd even toured a show during the holidays. My darling daughter was already earning money, which was unexpected. But she was happy, and that made me happy.

Dylan ran to join his dad. They adored each other.

"Congrats," Lachlan said, looking at me. "I hear there's a wedding planned, and that you've got another on the way."

I looked at Orlando, and he returned a wink.

Although it didn't come as a surprise to Orlando, it came as a surprise to me that we were still thick five years later.

We'd settled into a good life together. When Orlando wasn't in his studio making music, he was surfing, playing with Dylan, or in the bedroom playing with me. He was insatiable.

On special occasions, I'd tantalize him in my tiny nurse's uniform, which I'd kept as a reminder of our lusty past.

Dylan took after his dad musically. He had his own little guitar and showed early signs of talent. That's when he wasn't tumbling and cartwheeling around the house.

The Artefactory kept us busy. We ran shows monthly, and Clint was still there creating his sexy but strange furniture and coming up with weirdly magical concepts that seemed to bring in a young, groovy crowd.

Miranda stuck to what she knew best, consorting with established art buyers that kept the gallery financially viable. The young art lovers gave it that edge of excitement and buzz.

I couldn't have been happier, especially with Orlando cheering me on by my side. Loving me and making me see stars.

And to think, one wild night, it started in Venice.

THE END